Raven-Scar the town that never was

Book one of the Harry and Tina mysteries

Robert Marshall

Copyright © Robert Marshall 2011

First Edition 2011

Second Edition 2013

All rights reserved. No part of this publication may be reproduced, stored in a retrieval system, or transmitted, in any form or by any means, electronic, mechanical, photocopying, recording or otherwise, without the prior permission of the copyright owner.

Robert Marshall has asserted his right to be identified as the author of this work in accordance with the Copyright, Designs and Patents Act 1988

Second edition published

By

O'Dwyer and Marshall

Dedication

To my grandchildren James and Jade

Preface

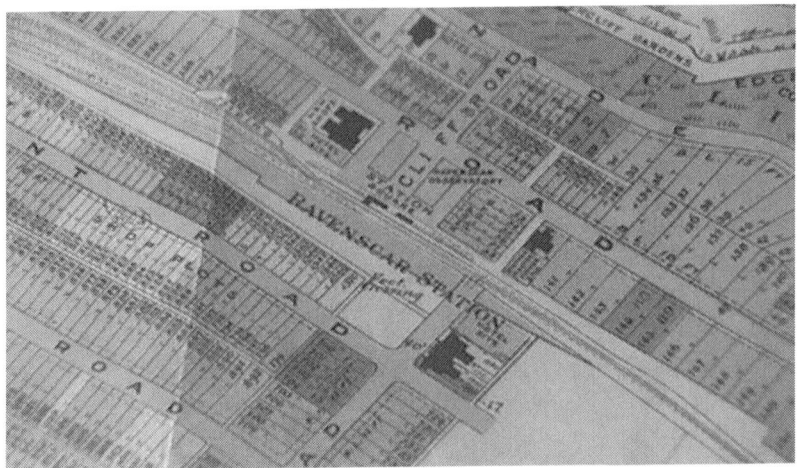

At the beginning of this century a Victorian entrepreneur decided that a town should be developed around the village then known as Peak .

A railway line was being built to link the towns of Scarborough and Whitby, and Peak was the central point. Roads were built, sewers were laid and plots of land sold. The plan was badly researched as the route to the shore is precarious and the area, though beautiful, is very exposed. The building company folded in 1913 having built less than a dozen houses. Peak was re-named Ravenscar. The disused station platform stands next to the old railway line which is now a bridleway.

This, then, is the background to the story "Raven-Scar or The town that never was"

Robert Marshall

2011

Above the station and tea rooms as they were in 1908
And below as looks in 2013

Above: the Railway tunnel at Ravenscar whilst still used and below a picture taken in 1970 shortly after it was decommissioned.

Raven-Scar or the town that never was

CHAPTER 1

Harry was hot; very hot. The climb up the old rail track to Ravenscar was longer than he remembered. Maybe he was getting too old to ride all this way but at thirteen he did not think he could get away with such an excuse. He looked at his twelve year old companion who looked cool and not really bothered at all about the cycle ride. As far as Tina was concerned there was very little of a problem, even though they had ridden from Scarborough.

As they rode past Staintondale they met up with a few horse riders, enjoying the quiet of the countryside. Horses and riding was something Tina really, really enjoyed when she had the time, but school and homework plus piano lessons took a lot of time out of a week.

At least she and Harry could get out on their bikes. And at this time of year it was an exciting ride on the rail track. One didn't know what to expect; it could be walkers, horses and their riders, mountain bikers and the occasional motorcycle would be ridden along the cinder surface. The latter was against the law but some people ignored laws, until their misdeeds were found out and then the magistrate would dish out community punishment.

On the odd occasion, they had met up with the local Staintondale Hunt. The hunting horn would proclaim the presence of horse and rider. Today the Staintondale hunt was out and coming down the track towards them, at this time the hounds and horses were all together. Hounds out in front, their noses to the ground, horses and riders closely following.

The hound's with tongues lolling, moved swiftly and silently as they approached. The hounds parted and swept around the two cyclists like a flowing tide. The Huntsmen were different of course they assumed everybody would move out of their way. Not this time. The two of them had decided not to move but to stay put and to heck with the Huntsmen.

They unfortunately ran foul of a large gent on an even larger grey horse. When he saw that the two children were not moving from their position raised his riding crop.

'Get out of the way damn you. Move. Come on or you'll feel this.' He swung the crop as if to slash at them with it.

Harry was not perturbed. 'If you do I'll call the Police on my mobile, see I've got it here?' Harry raised his hand with his phone in it. The large gent harrumphed, called them some words which they had never heard before, dug his heels in and trotted off after the other riders who by now were quite some distance down the track.

'I don't think he would have used that crop do you?' asked Tina.

'Not really. I think he was bluffing. Still, why do we have to move out of their way? We have as much right as they to stay on the cinders. I'm not riding into the banking just for them. Have you seen the depth of that ditch? And I'll bet its full of water, stagnant water at that.' Harry was correct. The ditch was as he said, wet and smelly. 'Anyway I'm absolutely boiling. How come girls don't sweat as much as boys? I can feel sweat running down my back. I hope the café is open when we get to Ravenscar, I could drink a well dry I'm so thirsty. But I'll settle for a drink of coke preferably. Do you want anything Tina?'

'A coke will do very well. What time is it Harry? We should be getting back'

'Mmm! 4-30, come on time for a drink anyway. Race you.'

'Do you know when you said why don't girls sweat? My grandma always said that "horses sweat, men perspire and ladies glow." Tina pushed down on the bike's peddles as she accelerated away from Harry.

'So, what does that mean? You either sweat or you don't?' Harry called as Tina shot away from him.

Tina shouted into the wind so that Harry could hear her.

Raven-Scar or the town that never was

'It's just something she always said I suppose, when she was a little girl in the 1940s. Probably that was just a figure of speech, like we say hiya, something like that. I sincerely hope we can get something to drink Harry? I'm really thirsty now. Come on, there's the old platform.'

The tiny village of Ravenscar was balanced on top of the cliffs between Whitby and Scarborough. The Raven Hotel stood on the very tip of those cliffs. Anyone with vertigo would have a hard time looking out of the windows at the rear.

Ravenscar would have been a town if developers had had their way. Unfortunately as in 2009 the financial situation in the 1900s was just as of now, in crisis. People were sold plots of land with the intention of speculators cashing in on building a town to rival the two towns either side of Raven-Scar. It came to nought. Planning permission and all sorts of other problems gave false hope to the holders of deed to property. With the whole thing becoming like a pack of cards and with that the enterprise came to nought. The problem for future developers was that over time the deeds to land became lost, forgotten or people just gave up hope. Land that had been bought was still owned by someone. In the end it had proved too difficult to try to find either deeds or original family owners.

Now, the few houses that had been built took on an air of mystery. The cliff tops still had the original roads and drains laid down so long ago. At times it could feel slightly eerie especially when a 'sea fret' surrounded the few houses that stood near the old station. These were built as show houses for speculators to look at and imagine what the developers had in mind. Fortunately for Harry and Tina one of the buildings was open as a café, much to their delight.

They walked the last few fifty metres or so.

'Harry do you think it's getting colder?' Tina asked.

'Mmm, and it looks like a sea fret is building up and it looks very dark up there beyond the platform. I think the tunnel is not very far away up there, you wouldn't know it though. Now you can hardly see beyond the platform.' Harry shivered; it was getting colder. 'Come on maybe a coffee or hot chocolate will warm us up?'

They ran towards the café, chaining their two bikes to some old cast iron railings before entering. The door closed behind them; they waited until their eyes became accustomed to the gloom.

CHAPTER 2

'It looks a bit old fashioned, look at the lamps? I'm sure they are gas lights.' Harry pointed to the wall lights.

'Gas? Why gas? It must be a power cut or something. Did they used to have gas lamps Harry? They must have been pretty dangerous.'

'Yes years ago. I mean the only gas lamps I've seen were in my gran's caravan, they ran off of a gas bottle. She lit them with a match, and she would turn the little tap on and the light went 'pop' as it lit. I mean they were OK in the caravan but I wouldn't say any good in a house we can hardly see in here. Anyway let's see if we can get that coffee or something. It looks like the counter is over there.'

Walking to the highly polished dark wooden counter it appeared to be deserted. A shiny brass bell stood to one side of the old fashioned till. Harry gave the top of the bell a tap. The bell rang louder than he thought it would. A voice from somewhere behind the mirrored glass back on the opposite side to the counter called out.

'Ada see to customers will tha?' A young woman entered from behind the mirrors. Tina was slightly surprised to see that Ada was not dressed in anything like normal clothing. She wore a white apron over a long slightly billowy dress which nearly touched the floor. On her dark curly hair she had a white hat, which Tina knew to be called a mop cap, a bit old fashioned she thought but I suppose something has to be done to attract customers; there was nothing else here in Ravenscar that she knew about. No amusements like Scarborough and more to the point, no beach either, and besides, it fitted in very well with the old fashioned décor. She rather liked the place.

Smiling, the young woman wiped her hands on a towel. 'Sorry love's we were a bit busy round t' back, we've just 'ad a load of coal delivered, and it's a bit mucky. Now what can I get thee?'

'Two cokes please?' said Harry.

'Eh, now what does tha' want wi' coke lad will tha eat it or tek it 'ome?' Ada laughed at her joke.

'No we want to drink it.' Harry sounded a little puzzled.

'Drink it? Nay lad tha' can't drink coke. What's up wi' thee? George come in 'ere I've got two weird people 'ere, so I 'ave.'

A large man came from the same place as Ada. He was tall and wore a leather apron, and trousers held up with a pair of braces. A large moustache drooped on either side of his face and his dark hair had long bushy side burns. Tina thought he looked like he had come off of an old film set.

'Nah then what's up?' His hands were covered in black dust, wiping them on a towel which was covered in the same black dust.

'These two want two glasses of coke' said Ada, her eyebrows rising.

'Some kind of joke then lad is it?'

'No! We want a drink of coke or something. I mean if you haven't got any coke then can we have some coffee or hot chocolate please? We've ridden all the way from Scarborough on the old rail track and now we want a drink that's all.' Harry was becoming a bit apprehensive about this.

'Well if tha wants a drink why din't tha say so?' George was looking closely at the two cyclists.

'And what does tha mean tha's ridden on t'old rail track? Tha'll 'ave to be careful t'trains don't run into thee. Anyrode, where as t' left 'osses?'

'Osses? Oh you mean horses.'

'Ay. 'Osses.'

Raven-Scar or the town that never was

'Oh we didn't come on 'osses, I mean horses; we came on our bikes. We did see the hunt horses out, running down the track to....' Harry was cut short in his explanation.

'Just a minute lad. What does tha mean 'unt 'osses. Yon 'unt in't out today and they'd be damn stupid to ride down rail track wi' trains running like.'

'Trains don't run down the track not now. Are you pulling our legs? It's not funny being refused anything. We thought this was a café but so far you have refused us a simple thing like a drink of Coco-Cola. What if I asked for a Kit-Kat? Would you refuse us that too?'

'I dun't like the tone of tha' voice young man. If you and your friend are 'aving a joke wi' us that's alreet, we understand, but joke's gone on long enough na' so come on what does tha want serious like?'

The man called George was beginning to sound rather annoyed and perplexed. 'And another thing yon young lass shouldn't be going ar'and dressed like that,' pointing to the shorts and top that Tina was wearing. 'It's not reet that young lass should walk around like that showing off her legs. It's not seemly.'

'What's wrong with Tina's shorts? She always wears them when we go for a ride.' asked Harry.

'Well that's up to thee like but if Constable sees thee, 'e'll probably tek thee straight 'ome and lay law down wi' your parents, now two cups of tea. That'll cost thee fivepunce,' Harry put five pence on the counter and turned to give Tina one of the cups of tea. 'Ere' what's this tha's given me? This in't right.'

'Yes it is. You asked for five pence. I must say that's very cheap for two teas, but you asked for five pence and I have given you five pence.' Harry was becoming more and more puzzled. Tina was moving closer to him so that she whispered in his ear.

'Give him the money Harry and let's go. There is something wrong about this place.'

Harry whispered back.

'I have given him five pence, look two, two pence's and a one pence. That's all he asked for.'

George was glaring at the two youngsters, and then he shouted.

'Ada, go and fetch Constable. 'E should be on't station.'

Ada went out of the door. Tina and Harry tried to leave the same way, but George stood in front of them barring their way. Ada returned in a few minutes with a Policeman.

Harry stared and nudged Tina she looked at the figure standing in the door way. He was a tall man with his helmet on; his jacket had a wide leather belt with, as the two gazed at it, a truncheon - an old fashioned truncheon - and from his top jacket pocket a whistle hung on a chain. His top lip sported a moustache similar to the one George wore and he had long sideburns. In the gloom he looked rather formidable. Tina moved closer to Harry. The Policeman moved further into the room and in the brighter light he did not look quite so formidable. Harry did notice an odd look about the Constable; his collar ended high up on his neck with no room for a neck-tie. In fact his appearance was very similar to the figures of Police through the ages he had seen in York Museum. And if Harry's memory was correct this Constable looked as if he came from about 1900 –well before World War WI.

Still, it must be some form of fancy dress decided Harry. He was beginning to feel uncomfortable that something was not quite right, as if he and Tina had stepped into a film set. Of course that was it! These people were actors the Heartbeat series, or something similar TV programme. Harry had the explanation.

Raven-Scar or the town that never was

CHAPTER 3

'Now then George, what's up this time?' The Policeman looked at the two cyclists. 'Is them your bikes out there?' pointing to the door.

'Y-yes they are.' Tina spoke for the two of them.

'Can't say I've seen any like them afore; so George, tell me what this is all about will you?'

'Aye, ah will an all. These two came in 'ere and asked for two glasses of coke. I mean does that sound reet to thee, Cyril?'

Cyril smiled. 'Sounds like a joke to me Harry.'

'Oh aye. Some joke when they tried to pay me in foreign money.'

'What do you mean foreign money? That's not foreign it's English money.' Harry was annoyed now. This was really very peculiar.

'Now then lad, tell me your name and the name of this lass here. And tell her to put her clothes on. I'll not have this sort of conduct here. Come on now lass, get dressed.' 'I AM dressed. This is how I dress.' said Tina.

Cyril eyed her up and down. Tina was tall for her age. Long, blonde hair hung down her back, long slim legs showed below her shorts and her halter top showed her bare brown arms. Feet firmly in her trainers, she was a normal looking twelve year old and definitely firm friend of Harry.

The Policeman took off his jacket and draped it around Tina's shoulders. 'I'll talk to you later young lady. Go and sit over there. Now lad, what're your names, you and this lass here?' He took out a notebook and pencil and licking the pencil point he started to write, looking at Harry. 'Name lad? Come on'

'My name is Harry Mortimer and she is Tina Whitely. We are both from Scarborough and we rode our bikes up the old railway track. Look, this is all very silly. Why won't he take our money? He,' pointing at George, 'asked for five pence and I must say that's rather too daft for words nobody charges five pence for two cups of tea unless this is a charity shop. Oh crikey! Is that it? This is all a game for charity. That's why you are dressed like you are. I get it now. You're collecting for the hospice or something, Pudsey Bear or something like that. I should have known' Harry looked across at Tina and grinned.

'That's it Tina they are collecting for charity, but why so serious? Come on. Tell us which charity it is? My mum works at the Hospice but she would have told me about a-n-y c-h-a-r-i-t-y.'

Harry stopped talking when he saw the puzzled look on the faces of the three adults.

'Not a charity?'

George shook his head, 'Charity begins at 'ome lad not 'ere.'

Cyril stopped writing and took the coins from the top of the counter. He looked closely at them.

'George come over here and take a look at these coins?' George moved closer to the Policeman who pointed to the head of the Queen on the two pence piece. 'The inscription says 'Queen Elizabeth the Second D.G REG. F D. Look at the date George? 2009 and look at the back - that's the Prince of Wales feathers. I know that as they were my regiment's colours. And see the words two pence with a two at the bottom.' Turning to Harry he asked him. 'Tell me son - what's the name of the King?'

'King? We don't have a King. We have the Queen as it says on the money. Elizabeth. She has been the Queen for a very long time since 1953 I think. Before her it was her father King George the Sixth, and before that his brother Edward the eighth who abdicated. Before that I think it was George the fifth. I'm not too sure about that Tina will know.'

Raven-Scar or the town that never was

'Yes. I think it was George the fifth. Now it's, oh, I'm not too sure, is it Edward the seventh? Why what's the problem?'

Cyril held up the two pence coin and looked very closely at the two children. 'I'm going to ask you very seriously to answer my question truthfully, because something very odd is happening here. Who are you and where do you come from?'

'We told you. Our names are Harry and Tina we come from Scarborough and we rode up the old rail track to get here. Listen if you don't believe me go and look at our bikes they are covered in mud from the track.'

'I have looked at those bikes, and they are very strange looking to me. Nothing like the bike I ride.'

At that moment a train whistle blew, startling Tina and Harry.

'That's a train whistle.' said Harry. 'That's not possible.'

'Why not? The station is only a few yards from here?' George was getting tired of this. These two young con men were trying to pass forged coins onto him and those coins looked nothing like normal pennies or half-pennies. It was about time Cyril took these two down to the Police station. The sound of the train was louder now as if it was coming to a halt. They could hear steam being blown off. 'It's a long drag from Staintondale up to 'ere and train stops for a quarter hour for driver to 'ave a cuppa.'

'But that's impossible. The trains don't run anymore.' Tina now was very frightened. Something really weird was happening. 'They stopped trains running on this line in 1964. A man called Beeching stopped lots of trains running and this is one of them. The trains do not run to Whitby any more. Look. you've had your joke and just let us get on our bikes and go home. Our parents will be wondering where we are.

The café door swung open to allow two men into the room, both of them had grimy overalls on and were wearing greasy flat hats that at one time had been smart. Both had grimy faces and the older man had a neckerchief around his neck. Both had very heavy looking boots on with shiny fronts to them. Tina saw that the shiny fronts where made of metal, it showed through where the leather had worn away.

'Gi' us two pots of brew George lad. We're fair dying of thirst. Albert 'as burnt 'is 'and. 'Ave you ow't for a burn Ada?' Ada said she had and disappeared around behind the counter coming back with a bowl of warm water and some liniment, she dressed Albert's hand.

'Silly bugger tried to open t'fire box door wi'art a cloth on 'is 'and!'

'Alright Jack. You've said your piece. Now shut thi gob and less of it. By 'eck Ada, tha's looking reet lovely to neet, ah could tek thee for a walk if tha liked.' Albert stood very little chance of 'tekking Ada 'art'. She told him so. 'Well, any road, this tea is just reet. Ta love.'

'Ada love,' Jack said, 'as tha got any matches? We 'ave to leet lamps in carriages and we 'aint got any bloody matches. Forgot all abar't 'em.' Ada handed him a box of Swan Vestas. 'Eh, ta lass. Thanks very much. Come on thee. 'Urry up wi'yon tea.' Jack reminded Bert.

Harry and Tina were sitting down holding hands both by now very confused and a little bit scared. This was becoming a nightmare. They remained silent while the two, Albert and Jack, had finished their mug of tea. Both men started for the door. Albert blew a kiss to Ada and ran out of the door before she could throw her cloth at him.

'Tarra, see you in about two hours,' both men left the room. Harry and Tina soon heard a train whistle and the chuffing and puffing of an old steam engine. With the clanking of carriages and the squeal of iron wheels as they started to turn. They heard a whistle being blown and the train started moving.

'Not many passengers to-neet,' Ada noticed. 'Percy 'as teken five on em t' Hotel. Pity, we could do wi someone calling 'ere. We 'avent 'ad anybody for a couple of neets. Nay well it'll pick up next week when kids are on 'oliday. Now

Raven-Scar or the town that never was

what's going to 'appen to these two Cyril? They've given us foreign money and that's like stealing.'

Cyril stood up and made for the door.

'Come outside all of you. Come on I want to show you something.' They all trooped outside. Harry and Tina looked in amazement at what they saw: the three houses that were there when they first went into the café were now surrounded by buildings all looking reasonably new. In front of the café was a small grassed area which had an oval cobbled road surrounding it? Looking to their right they gazed in astonishment at the station building built of wood with steps leading up to a large open passage with a ticket office clearly to be seen. A horse and cart rumbled past the bottom of the lane going in the direction that they had ridden up some time ago. The chilling strange mist had dispersed or gone somewhere else, at least they didn't shiver as they had done.

'Frank going t' coal yard.' explained George. 'Look Cyril, why does tha want us out 'ere like?'

'I want to show you the two bicycles these two youngsters said they rode here from Scarborough. Look have you seen anything like these before?' Cyril pointed to Tina and Harry's mountain bikes. 'Now I've been riding a bike most of my life and I've never seen anything like these in all the time I've been riding. Have either of you two?' He asked George and Ada.

'Never see 'owt like them afore. Can they be ridden? They don't look too good to me? They're not Raleigh's that's certain. What's that one called - a Specialized? And t'others a Marin. Never 'eard of any name like that. Look at the saddle and what's them things there?' he pointed at the water bottles on the frame.

'And are those gears or something? Nay I've not seen 'owt like 'em. No never. Seems like they're circus bikes like as not? Are they circus bikes lad?' Harry could not speak. What he saw when he looked around him both frightened and astonished him. Tina was holding his hand very firmly so firmly that he thought his fingers would be bloodless.

'Why do you think they are circus bikes?' Harry wanted to know.

'What George means young man, is that what you call bicycles are not bicycles. look over there that's my bike. The one issued by the Police Force in Whitby and let me assure you it is nothing like what you are calling a bicycle is it, mmm?'

Cyril, although a member of the Police Force, was also a keen astronomer. A large telescope stood in the back room of the Police House overlooking the cliff tops where on a clear night he could star-gaze to his heart's content. Also he was a keen reader of science fiction - Jules Verne and H G Wells. He knew it was impossible but there was a niggling thought at the back of his mind. These two young people were definitely not having any kind of joke with them; they looked too frightened now that they had come outside of the Station Café.

'Look George if it's alright with you I'd like to take these two down to the Station and ask 'em a few questions, alright?' George said he had no objection to that but he would like to have his fivepunce for the tea. Cyril brought out from his pocket a handful of coins and counted out five pence. 'Come on both of you. Follow me and bring those machines along with you.

Raven-Scar or the town that never was

CHAPTER 4

Harry fumbled for the key for the bike lock while the Constable unchained his bike which looked very old fashioned to Harry and Tina. They all started to walk away from the café and turned left at the bottom of the lane. When the two children turned the corner they gasped at what lay before them. Houses stretched into the mist on both sides of the cobbled road. A few shops were all open, Tina read the name, 'The Ship', on a public house. 'This is impossible Tina there's nothing here at Ravenscar only a few houses. What's happening I thought when we were in the café that we had stumbled into a film set or something like that but this is impossible?' Tina was shivering with fright.

'Harry I'm very scared. All I want to do is go home. Can't we phone? Please use your mobile.'

'Yes of course I'd forgotten about that,' he said. Taking his mobile out of his pocket he flipped the lid up and nearly dropped the phone. 'Shit there's no signal Tina. It's worked before. Look it isn't even registering. There's nothing on the dial at all.'

'Please Harry try the numbers?' pleaded Tina.

Harry dialled his home number. Nothing. Then he tried Tina's. Nothing. Nothing at all, not even any signal on the navigation section. Only the game section was lit up. By now both of them were too frightened to think of what to do.

Cyril looked behind him to see the two young people looking into an object that Harry had in his hand. He beckoned for them to hurry up as he turned and walked steadily away from them. Tina and Harry jumped on to their bikes and pushed hard and fast on the pedals, they rode over the cobbled road and the shaking and jarring did not trouble them all they wanted to do was get away from this place.

As they passed the Policeman he looked startled and shouted for them to stop, but no way were they going to do that. They rode harder, standing on the pedals so as to get as much speed as they could, speeding into the misty distance and coming to an abrupt halt at some cross-roads. Still the houses stretched before them, extending both left and right and all the way to the cliff top.   To them, the road in front should be the road back to Scarborough. Here there were more houses, a sort of garage with a petrol pump down one side, more shops and two more public houses.

Finally Cyril caught up with them.

'What is the matter with you two? I told you to follow me and I mean follow me. Come along.'

The Policeman was angry as he turned his bike around and continued walking back the way they had all ridden.

Tina and Harry followed too scared to do any other.

After only a few yards along the road they turned onto a side road. Tina noticed the name 'The Crescent' and the second building had a notice above the door. 'Police Station Raven-Scar section'. The word Police was written on a glass lamp that hung over the door. Cyril opened the door and pushing his bike up the few steps he motioned for the other two to do the same.

Once inside the Police Station Cyril unbuttoned his jacket, the one which he had placed over Tina's shoulders, and handed it to her with the instructions that she 'cover herself up'. He went into a small room that led off of the main section of the Police house. As he did so he called out to Tina and Harry and told them to sit down. He returned with a tray on which were three mugs, a teapot and also a plate of biscuits. Pouring the tea out he offered mugs to his 'prisoners' which they accepted with gratitude. Both by now were hungry and thirsty.

Raven-Scar or the town that never was

The Policeman sat down on a large comfy looking chair and leant closer to the two children. He looked at them with an intense gaze.

Taking a long drink from his mug, Cyril placed it back onto the tray which he had placed on the counter of the station house. This was his work place and he had a very uncomfortable feeling that what was to be said next was alarming to all three of them.

'Now Harry, I want you to tell me what the date is and what the year is, can you think straight enough to answer me correctly?'

Harry nodded holding his mug in his slightly shaky hands. He whispered at first then clearing his throat he spoke clearly.

'It is the fourteenth of August and the year is 2009'. Looking at his watch he also said. 'And the time is 17-45.'

'Let me 'ave a look at that thing please Harry?' said Cyril, pointing to the watch. Harry undid the strap and passed the watch over.

'What the heck?!' a startled exclamation as the watch lit up when he pressed one of the three buttons.

Handing it back he asked. 'How does it work Harry lad?' Harry pushed the buttons in sequence and as the display went through its programme the Constable nodded at each different display.

Cyril took another drink from his mug looking at Tina and raising his eyebrows at her in a questioning manner. Tina nodded her head in agreement with Harry only she did whisper her confirmation. Cyril stood up from his chair and walked backwards and forwards across the Police Station floor. He went behind the counter and took a calendar from the wall, which he offered it to Harry and Tina. Harry's hand trembled as he took the calendar and he nearly dropped it onto the floor when he saw the date at the top. 1909 it stated. *The same day and the same month but one hundred years in the past.*

Harry looked at Tina who had gone sheet white and he saw tears in her eyes he stood up and put his arm around her shoulder. He could feel her shiver as she held back tears and looking at him, Tina tried to speak slowly.

'Harry that's impossible, it can't be that date? How can it be? I don't understand. How can it be a hundred years ago? Harry, tell me it isn't so please. This is a nightmare and I'm very frightened.'

She gave a sob as Harry tightened his arm around her but he had no answer except that they had ridden into a nightmare.

If the calendar in his hand was correct then they had come back in time one hundred years. Harry had to think clearly about what they had seen over the past two hours. His head reeled with the nonsense of it all. It was not possible to go back in time. There must be a simple explanation. And the only one that came to his mind was that they had simply stumbled onto a film set. That was all he could think of.

Looking at the tall figure of the Constable, he stammered a response.

'It's not possible. It can't be 1909 - it just can't. Look, I have my mobile phone here and I can ring my parents... Oh! My goodness, I can't. If it's true, mobile phones did not exist a hundred years ago did they? And what's more, both my parents would not have been born. I'm not too sure whether my grandparents had been born then Cyril. Sorry but can I call you that, officer seems so, so inept? I can't get my head round this at all. If this place really is Raven-Scar when was it built?'

'Built? I don't really know when. But I think it was around 1889 or thereabouts when the land was sold off and companies started building houses. Then in 1902 they built a pier out into the sea and a harbour before that - quite a big harbour as well. Not as big as Scarborough but big enough to take trawlers and so forth: some steam trawlers

Raven-Scar or the town that never was

use it now for landing their catches. Why did you ask that question Harry?'

Harry still had his arm around Tina who had started to listen carefully to the conversation.

In a small voice Tina spoke.

'Because this place was never built, it's called the Town that Never Was. Oh, the land was offered for sale and some of the roads were built along with the station and a few houses. But that was all. It doesn't exist, it never did. More to the point, it most certainly does not have a pier or harbour come to that.

If I remember reading about it at school the main problem was lack of money. Also it was not possible to have a beach. There was no sand and the rocks around the cliff bases saw to that. So the whole project was abandoned and the plots of land that were sold just became farms again. It doesn't exist. Harry please, help me, are we going mad or something? We are in a place that doesn't exist. How can that be Harry? Tell me we aren't going mad, that it's some kind of nightmare dream.'

Harry could not help his companion. He could only hold her tightly as she trembled with shock.

'Alright Tina, it's alright' Cyril knelt before her.

'Sit down Harry lad. There has to be an explanation. Here, drink this tea lass. We have to give this some serious thought and for your information I don't think you are going mad. Well no more than I when I think about it. So come on dry those lovely eyes and let's do some thinking. My wife will be home soon then we can have dinner and a long chat. She's on the next train from Whitby and is a steady lass.'

As he mentioned Whitby, Tina stiffened as if in shock but she calmed down when Harry put his arm around her shoulder again.

CHAPTER 5

The conversation had to start somewhere and as Cyril was a Policeman and an adult he felt it was up to him to try to make some sense of the situation.

'Now as I see it there has to be an explanation. Something quite bizarre is happening and I have to confess I'm a bit frightened and unsure myself, come to think of it. I read a book a while ago by a man called H G Wells. It's supposed to be what they call science fiction or something like that. There's a magazine called Future Stories, and it's something I haven't read, but this story was called "The Time Machine" and it described journeys into the future and into the past. All in the imagination of this man Wells. This is the problem as I see it. And it's a big problem. The problem is that you say this place does not exist when quite clearly it does, or I wouldn't be here would I? No more would George and Ada be here, or the train or the town. I agree this cannot be happening normally, but what if something not normal had happened to you.

As you say, you rode your strange bicycles along the extinct rail track; and I have to admit that when I looked at your money I felt a queer feeling come over me; now I can't explain it but when I read the inscription and handled the coins I knew something very queer had happened. I must confess to you that as a Constable I handle a lot of counterfeit money.' Cyril gave a short guffaw. 'Ha-ha, you wouldn't believe the sort of things that thieves get up to! But your coins felt somehow right. I say I can't explain it, it's just, well, words fail me at the moment. And your clothes Tina; no girl your age would go around dressed like you are they would be arrested for displaying too much. Not even when bathing would women dress that way. And Harry,

Raven-Scar or the town that never was

what you are wearing are the same shorts that are for runners and athletes or footballers - not for walking around in.

Your cycles! They are nothing like mine nor any other that I know of so no wonder old George thought they were circus bikes. Your watch Harry, nothing like that exists to my knowledge. That thing you call a mobile it lights up how? Either you two are very accomplished actors with some funny gadgets or, well, what alternative answer is there?' Here Cyril paused shaking his head, then quietly he continued.

'Or you are what you say you are. Help me here please, if you think you are in a night-mare then I also am in one. My goodness this is incredible. As you say Tina, this can't be happening, but it is and come what we think, we have to find an answer.' He sat down looking at his two 'prisoners.' 'It looks like the impossible has happened how and why I have no idea.'

As he said this, the door opened and a woman stepped inside, short and dumpy, dark hair under a large floppy hat, a cape round her shoulders which she took off and shook the wet mist off of it. Her dress reached down to the floor and Tina saw that she wore boots with buttons up the side. She gasped when she saw the boots. They were the same type that she had seen in an old black and white photo of her great grandma. A stern face looking out onto a new medium of photography.

She spoke in a loud voice, 'Cyril I've got some lovely chops for dinner from the.... Oh sorry love. There you are. I didn't see you there. Hello. Who are these two young 'uns then?'

Cyril cleared his throat.

'It's a long story lass and somewhat complicated, and to be quite honest I don't know where to start. Look, let me make another pot of tea then I can tell you something very strange.'

'Oh! How strange? Nay lass,' she said as she noticed Tina. 'You look frozen dressed like that. Trust a man to not get you wrapped up proper like. I must say you look right bonny. Are they new types of knickers and vest? Nay how come you're dressed like that in broad daylight? Has this young man tried something on with you? If he has he'll be charged with assault. Cyril get me my dressing gown from behind bedroom door.' turning to look at Harry she continued. 'You sit right over there young man I'll have words with you later. I hope you haven't been misbehaving. Go on sit' Harry sat.

Tina couldn't help but laugh at the look on this woman's face.

'No, no Harry is my friend and I dress like this. He wouldn't do anything to hurt me we are just friends. And we rode our... well never mind Cyril will try to explain things.'

Cyril returned with a fresh pot of tea with more biscuits, setting the tray down on the counter once more. He left the room and returned with a dark blue floor length woollen dressing gown. He helped Tina into it then started to pour more tea as an afterthought he introduced his wife.

'Sorry you two this is my wife Agnes Whittaker, we've been married now for twenty years. Sit thisen down love have a cup of tea and let me get my thoughts right. Oh sorry this young lady goes by the name of Tina and this here is Harry. They came on their bicycles from Scarborough up the railway line.' He left the question hanging in the air.

'Oh, I see. Well that's no problem you said you had something to tell me?' Agnes placed her cup carefully on to a small side table and looked at her husband. 'Cyril are you daft or something you just said that they rode their bikes up the railway track. That is a very silly thing to do. Really you should have more sense than to do that at your age. Any road, why are you dressed like something from a stage show? I mean wearing shorts is not the done thing in this day and age unless you are running a race or something;

Raven-Scar or the town that never was

and Tina love, you really should not go around looking like that. It really is not seemly.'

'Just a minute dear, let me try to explain. But before I do these two will have to sleep here for to-night, they...' but before he could finish Agnes gasped.

'Oh, you poor dears you're 'omeless that's why you have no proper clothes of course you can sleep here.' Again she smiled, 'although it will have to be in a cell for you Harry we only have two bedrooms. Look loves I'll make some dinner then we can talk, poor dears. Cyril, why didn't you say they had no home?'

'Well they haven't here - that's very correct, yes alright love make some dinner I take it the chops will be enough for four?'

'Ee, well you know William he allus gives me good value he does, me being local Constable's wife like. Right it won't take me long. Cyril, have you finished your duties for to-day?'

'No I've the daily book to record in but it won't take me long. By the time you've got dinner I'll have finished. Was Whitby busy?'

'Ee, I'll say' Agnes spoke from the kitchen. 'Market day is always busy. There was a bit of trouble down on the docks though. A French boat wanted to land its catch. Those French fishermen think they can do what they like. They reckoned on't catch saying it would spoil afore they could get back to Le Havre. Well you know what it's like down there with foreign fishing boats. It was alright though. Mr Fellows and young Ernest sorted it out, won't be long now loves. Cyril, lay the table in here for me love.' Cyril closed his record book and went to do his wife's bidding.

Harry silently went to the counter. He beckoned for Tina to come to him. He opened Cyril's Day Book and the last entries read. "Mr Roland, farmer of Station Road reported two sheep missing; looks like poachers are back again. Shall have to report this to Whitby. Miss Walker, school teacher reports one of her pupils having a fit. Ambulance called and the boy is in the cottage hospital. Up-train driver reports a very thick mist approaching station. He says 'funny mist', I don't know what he means? Two children found passing foreign... This was crossed out and the writing continued. 'Two children found lost and asking directions, too late to return them to Scarborough they stay in Police Station for the night."

"Tomorrow's roster: Street patrol starting at 4am, return to Station House for breakfast. Continue with street patrol. At 10 a.m. shall go down to the harbour to enquire about French boats unlawfully landing a catch. Phone Whitby regarding sheep, may have to have assistance here in Raven-Scar if poachers are about."

'Look he doesn't know what to say about us being here?'

'Harry have you thought about how our parents will be thinking, if we stay the night here they will call out the Police for a search and how long will we be here? Harry they may think we have been kidnapped or worse murdered, and if they can't find our bodies, they will think we are dead, Harry I'm...'

'Tina don't get excited,' he pleaded.

'Harry we are in never, never land and you say, do not get excited? What else can I do? We may never return to our time or see our parents or friends again ever. Why did this happen to us? Tell me Harry why? I think we are crazy, and in a dream of sorts. Are we in a dream Harry?'

'I don't know I really don't I haven't got any answers to any questions. All I can remember is you asking me whether I thought it was getting colder. Then we went into that café. Just a minute, that train driver said that the mist was strange. How strange I wonder? And what else did he see? Tina he may give us a clue as to what happened to us?'

'Then why did his train not disappear. If the mist affected us, why not the train?'

Raven-Scar or the town that never was

'Probably too big' answered Harry. 'I'll ask Cyril if he knows the name of the train driver, then we can ask him, alright?' Tina nodded.

A shout from the kitchen asked the two children to "come for dinner you two." They went for dinner and by now both were so hungry they would have eaten anything.

CHAPTER 6

After a really tasty meal, and listening to Agnes regarding her day in Whitby, she said there where one or two new shops for her to scrutinise, possibly to buy something new for Cyril, a tie or a pair of collar studs. Agnes was one of those women that talked for other people "and did you know what she said, well I'll tell you what she said and it just isn't true what she told us about them". And so the meal passed without either Cyril, Tina nor Harry having to start an explanation.

It had to come though; Agnes could not be kept in the dark any longer. Cyril poured both himself and Agnes a glass of ale, giving Tina and Harry the choice of milk or lemonade. As the time was approaching 9-30 in the evening milk was preferred. They all settled in front of the fire in the kitchen, Cyril cleared his throat.

'Agnes love I've something very serious to tell you.'

'Well if it's to do with these two 'omeless youngsters then I reckon it is serious Cyril. Look, just a minute dear while I get something more comfortable for Tina to wear. I wonder if Harry can fit into a pair of your trousers Cyril. And see if you've got a spare pullover for t'lad; he looks a bit chilled to me.'

Agnes left the room returning with a long dress in black for Tina, it rustled like taffeta it did not fit of course as Agnes was rather stouter than the girl. Still it covered her from neck to toe and Tina felt more comfortable and much warmer. The Police Station was not the warmest of places, certainly not on a chilly foggy night such as was coming down now. Cyril handed a pair of trousers and a pullover which Harry noticed had a few holes in it. He turned the trouser bottoms up a few centimetres or he would have tripped over them. Tina looked at him and burst out

Raven-Scar or the town that never was

laughing. Harry looked at Tina in her large floppy dress which completely covered her and joined in the laughter. Gasping for breath they both sat down on some very uncomfortable kitchen chairs. Agnes and her husband looked on in amusement.

'Now then loves I know you look a little overdressed but we can get you something that will fit tomorrow from the church jumble sale. Mind you we'll have to be early or all the best stuff will go first.'

Harry and Tina started giggling again.

'Ssssorry Agnes. I can't help laughing at Tina it's the first time I've seen her dressed up.' Tina shot him a rude glance.

'Huh! You've some room to talk baggy britches.' This set them both off again, trying to stop they clapped a hand over their mouths Agnes looked so puzzled that they just could not look her in the face.

'Erm, love listen to me I've something very important and very strange to tell you. Harry and Tina are not from here.'

'Yes you told me they come from Scarborough; they rode here on their bikes. Didn't you say they rode up the railway track, how strange and very dangerous?'

'Not where they come from dear. They, erm, do come from Scarborough but, I mean, this is going to sound very silly and nonsensical and I really do not know where to start. Agnes love, these two come from another time. I am almost certain of that.'

'Time! What time? Of course they come from another time. How else would they get here? I don't think that's silly or strange at all. What I do think is very silly is riding a bike near the railway.'

'Agnes where they come from there is no railway, it isn't there at all. Well it was but it isn't now. And there's more; what they say is that this place does not exist, it never did. Harry said that the roads and drains were built along with a few houses but Raven-Scar was never built and I really don't know what else to say or do. Agnes, they are from another time - a sort of different world.'

'You mean they come from one of the villages out on the moor like Fylingdales or somewhere like that? I'm pretty certain they don't have a station there. Are you both from there?' Agnes turned to the two children with her question.

'No as Cyril said we come from Scarborough and we did ride our bikes along the old rail track.'

'Old rail track whatever do you mean this is the only one isn't it?'

'Yes and no Agnes, it did exist but it doesn't now it was taken away a long time ago in 1964 I think.'

Agnes stood up.

'Cyril, have these two escaped from an asylum? Is that what you want to tell me? If they have I think we should lock them in one of the cells until the authorities come for them. Cyril come on love, take the boy and I'll take the girl. Now come on love don't be frightened we will soon have you back with your friends. Oh my goodness what have I said?' Tina and Harry burst out laughing again thinking that both of them escaping from an asylum was funny, and just tickled them and started them both off laughing it sounded so funny?

'Agnes please sit down and listen to me. They are not loonies, they are two normal young people, of that I am sure. It is that they have been tricked in time and something happened to them as they came into the café near the station. Look this is the money they gave to George. Well you know George! He sent Ada to find me and wanted to charge them with theft. I took them away sharpish because I felt something odd about them. I mean look at their clothes closely I mean have you ever seen materiel like that before and Harry, let Agnes look at your watch and that other thing, that phone thing. Look. NO! Dear, don't press anything. Let Harry do it.'

Raven-Scar or the town that never was

Harry brought his chair nearer to the doubting woman. As he showed her the mobile phone it rang; Harry nearly dropped it in his haste to answer.

'Hello! Mum! It's me Harry. Listen Mum we are alright. We are not where we should be...! Damn Tina, that was definitely my Mum. How did that happen? Now the signal has gone. Oh Tina, what's happened? For a moment there, I thought we had returned.'

'Try dialling your home number again.'

'It's no good. Look, the signal is non-existent like this place is supposed to be.'

'Harry lad, try to explain to Agnes what those things are. Calm down and take your time. This is going to be very, very difficult. If it's any consolation to you I think I believe you about what you are saying. Agnes, this is a watch that tells time, dates, adds things up and takes things away like sums at school. What else does it do Harry?'

'Well if you press this button here I can alter the time with this button, but my mobile will play games and such like. Oh I'm sorry, this is a telephone. It's called a mobile because I can carry it around with me and it works off of a battery that I have to charge up occasionally with a charger, which would be pretty useless now even if I had it. The watch also works off a battery and it will last for about two years and...'

'Stop! Please, I don't understand a word you are saying. Cyril please put them in one of the cells and telephone Whitby. Get in touch with Mr Fellows. Get him to send a carriage for them and let's be sensible. I have never heard such a story. These two are from a circus or something. Look at what they are telling us and showing us that thing he calls a telephone why it's sheer nonsense. Anybody can tell that it is not a telephone: and to say he can use it and carry it around with him is pure humbug. Now come on young lady this is for your own good I thought you were peculiar when I saw you had taken all your clothes off. Come on Cyril get hold of that lad before he gets out of the door.'

'Agnes, please, you're getting hysterical. Listen to me and listen to them. Let them tell you themselves and please sit down and let go of the girl.'

Cyril guided Tina to her chair and sat her down. Harry was still standing ready to either dash for the door or push Agnes away from him.

'Sit down Harry lad. Let's be sensible and calm down so we can maybe make some sort of sense out of the situation, but for the life of me I don't know what.' Harry sat down waiting until Agnes had been seated by her husband.

Cyril patted his wife's hand and handed her another glass of ale, which Agnes drank straight away. She leaned back in the chair with a bemused look on her pink face. Harry thought that at one time she would have hit him, thinking he was dangerous and an escaped loony from the lunatic asylum. Harry also thought there must have been plenty of people in those places for Agnes to get so upset. She was also not able to understand what he wanted to show her. He realised that the few items of his were just too technical for her to understand. In 1909, batteries, such as the ones powering his watch and phone could not possibly exist and it would be seventy years before they did. The same with his, and Tina's clothing. These items were made of man-made materials - nylon and Gore-Tex and not until the 1960s did this sort of material become available for clothing. And for both of their bikes, the metal used in the manufacturing was something far ahead in years. This was definitely going to be a very difficult time. It was also a very different time and century, and the items that he and Tina had with them, would they be invented in another time?

Raven-Scar or the town that never was

CHAPTER 7

The following morning as they ate breakfast cooked by Agnes, she began to quiz her husband, why this and why that? Are they really telling the truth? Not from this world indeed! Her husband may be a Constable but he didn't know everything, and these two were definitely fibbing.

Cyril left the kitchen and returned with a small hard backed book, handing it to his wife he asked her to look at the title.

'You know I don't read your books Cyril. Most of them are untrue and not what I would call good reading. They're not like the Bronte's at all; I mean look at this title 'The Time Machine' who is H G Wells anyway?'

'No love. Read what's on the cover page.'

"A story of the future, of time and space." Agnes read it out loud.

'So what has that got to do with these two?' pointing at Harry and Tina, and then she burst out laughing. 'Nay Cyril the next thing you are going to tell me is that they come from sometime in the future. Cyril love, it's simply not possible. Really, the idea of time travel this chap Wells wrote about has put some very silly ideas into your head, and what was that other book by that man Jules something or other?'

'Jules Verne.'

'Yes that's him you read something out to me from that book, something about a boat that goes under the sea. Cyril love, it's only fiction. You don't really believe in it do you? You're a Constable for goodness sake. Be sensible love. Ask Tina and Harry where they really come from?'

'I have asked them and they say they rode their bicycles up the 'old railway line'. Those are their exact words, 'the old railway line', and I'm beginning to believe them. I mean, why would they say that if they didn't mean it; and look at their cycles, I counted the gears on the back of one of them there are seven gear wheels on it with some sort of mechanism on it,' he turned to Harry. 'What does that do lad, I meant to ask you but it just went out of my mind?'

'It changes the ratio, look let me show you?'

Cyril and Agnes followed Harry and Tina to where the bikes were propped against the counter. Harry asked Tina to lift the rear wheel of his bike as he turned the pedals and twisted the gear grip on the handlebars. Cyril eyed the mechanism. With interest he followed precisely the way Harry moved the twist grip. Harry asked Tina to twist the other grip showing that the Derailleur moved the chain wheel gears. Cyril counted 21 gears altogether and to his mind this was engineering beyond his thinking. This was definitely science-fiction he thought. Fortunately it wasn't fiction. It was there in front of his eyes.

Tina put the bike down. Cyril looked at the brakes moving the lever and watching the callipers grip the wheel rims, he looked at his own Police issue machine noticing how the brakes worked and the single rear sprocket the brakes with their rods and 'stirrup' callipers, Harry's brakes were nothing like anything he had seen.

'Well I declare,' gasped Agnes. 'I must say, Cyril that it's a very clever device, but the Blacksmith out at Staintondale could make summat like that.'

'I very much doubt it dear, Tom is very good but this is something that looks like a scientist has made it.'

Harry interrupted, 'Not science Cyril, but machinery, special machinery, that works like a computer. Oh yes! Computers. Look, do I have to explain about that?'

'Not really Harry lad' Cyril grinned at Harry and patted Tina's hand. Turning to Agnes he said in a quiet voice. 'Agnes love I know I can't explain what has happened but I believe that it's true what these two are telling us. Harry, can you tell me what is going to happen next year?'

Raven-Scar or the town that never was

Tina said in a sharp voice. 'Harry you can't do that?'
'Why not?'
'Because you will make a difference in time.'
'I don't think so. Remember, this place in our time does not exist, the railway yes, but this town no, it never was, so how can I alter time?'
'Ask Cyril if there was ever a war called the Crimea or Boer. No, better still ask if the Napoleonic wars happened and oh, listen, Cyril when did the Battle of Trafalgar take place?'
'Well were there wars called that especially the Battle of Trafalgar?' asked Harry.
'Nay Harry lad. No there never was. If there had been it would have been in all the papers. The last war was the civil war something to do with the making of parliament. I do remember something about France but there never was a war with France. There was a treaty. Let me look in this book.'
Taking a small black book off of a shelf which held a dozen or so books Cyril leafed through the pages, 'yes I was right. A treaty was signed with the French. A trade treaty in 1805. I remember reading it at school, along with the British Empire. Aye, we've had wars of some sort there was trouble in India, and South Africa with Zulu's, and we had a bit of a skirmish with the Americans they didn't want to belong to the British Empire, so they kicked us out. Shame really because America by all accounts is a really go-ahead sort of place. I take it that in your time you have an America, and do you have wars?'
'Yes all of them along with two other world wars, and America is leading the world in most things. Although we British do invent things like jct planes and hovercraft and computers but they are relatively new, trains have been with us for over 150 years.
Tina we are not only back in time but in another dimension. Another world! The opposite of the one we come from. This is incredible. I remember in science Mr Walker

telling us that there has to be a fourth dimension. A time dimension, and we must have slipped through this dimension somehow; certain things happen at roughly the same time and date as in our world like the Battle of Trafalgar, and as Cyril just said in this world there was no battle but a trade treaty was signed. Our problem is how do we get back to our time?'

'Listen to me all of you. This is nonsense all this talk of time and space. Just because these two have funny bicycles doesn't mean they have travelled through time does it? There is a much simpler explanation; I'm just not sure what it is.' Agnes was flummoxed with all this talk of space and fourth dimension. She had never heard of this at her school, certainly not that she was taught science. Girls did not have that sort of teaching. Sewing and cooking, and the three Rs were all that she was taught. Science was definitely not for girls. And young children were still used in the huge mills as cheap labour even though an act in parliament forbade it. She asked Tina a question. 'If as you say both of you come from somewhere else tell me what you learned at school, mmm?'

Tina answered, 'In my school now I am learning maths, English, social history, geography, French, German, science and we do sports like swimming, football and if we want we can play rugby.'

'You play football?'

'Yes. Why not just because I'm a girl? That doesn't mean I can't play football or anything else come to that?'

'But football is a game for men,' exclaimed Agnes. 'Women don't play football?'

'Have women got the vote, same as men?' Tina asked Agnes, as she wanted to know.

Cyril answered Tina. 'No but there is a campaign for it to be passed in parliament, I don't think it will be allowed. Can women vote in your time?'

Raven-Scar or the town that never was

'Yes they have since, - I've forgotten when they got the vote - do you know Tina?' She shook her head. 'Sometime after the first world war I think' said Harry.

'The First world war good heavens, how many have you had?' Cyril found this fascinating; he had never heard such things.

'Two, the first lasting from 1914-18 and the second one from 1939-1945, in both wars we fought Germany.'

'Germany! You fought Germany?'

'Yes and Japan, they attacked America.'

'America! The Japanese attacked America that is unbelievable?'

'Cyril dear that is just as unbelievable as these two somehow coming back through time, IT IS NOT POSSIBLE. How many times do I have to say it? Listen dear we must think about what to do with these two children the more they say and the more I think about it I am sure they have escaped from somewhere. Think dear and look at them, why were they not fully-dressed when they went into Georges Café, tell me that? Then they spin this yarn and have you nearly believing them. It isn't true dear they are obviously deranged or simple minded. Look, do as I ask and phone through to Whitby see if any children matching their description have escaped from an asylum. Go on do it now dear and let's find out once and for all if these two are from were they are saying they are from. I do not for one minute believe their story, there has to be a simple explanation; go on dear phone Mr Fellows.'

'I can't do that now dear there'll only be a constable on duty. I'll have to telephone in the morning. Goodness me look at the time, it's far too late. Now what about these two for sleeping here? I think the lad will have to go in one of the cells and the young lady can sleep in the spare room' The arrangements were soon sorted out. Tina went to bed with a hot brick wrapped in a towel to keep her warm, while Harry had two blankets and a feather eiderdown for warmth.

Robert Marshall

The telling of tales had gone on for far too long; the Constable wanted to know more and more. He was intrigued by all that Tina and Harry were saying. Agnes brought sandwiches and soup, but the two 'time travellers' became too tired to say much more. They rolled into bed and cell; the same as the previous night; Tina to her bed, Harry to a cold dark cell, although he did have a candle at least it gave some light; they were both exhausted.

CHAPTER 8

Cyril was true to his word. The following morning, before anybody had eaten breakfast, he went to the phone which was on the counter. It was a tall black item with the dial on its base and the ear piece hanging from a hook. Lifting the telephone up and taking off the ear piece, Cyril dialled a number asking to speak to Sergeant Fellows. Listening for a few minutes, he replaced the ear piece on its cradle, saying that the Sergeant was not available he was out on an important case. Turning to Harry and Tina he suggested that they have a good look around Raven-Scar and do some exploring. Cyril had more or less convinced his wife that Harry and Tina were not escapees from an asylum but two young people who were frightened and bemused at their predicament.

'If as you say this place is none existent in your time then have a good scout around and look at the harbour and the shops.'

This seemed like a sensible idea to Tina and Harry. Agnes made up some sandwiches and told them they could buy some lemonade at one of the shops near the Raven Hotel. Harry reminded her that the money they had would not buy them anything. Agnes rummage in her purse and gave them both four large copper coins each. When asked what they were she explained that they were pennies and that a bottle of 'pop' would cost them half-pence. If they wanted to catch the bus to Robin Hood's bay the fare was two-pence return. Asked if they could use their bikes Cyril shook his head saying it wasn't advisable to ride anywhere on those machines people would ask questions.

Robin Hood's Bay sounded like a good idea, the charabanc, or 'bus' to them, was an open top vehicle not far removed from a lorry. And it gave an uncomfortable ride.

The few miles to the Bay, alighting from it at the top of the village, the two of them could see that Robin Hood's Bay was pretty much the same as in their own time and world of 2009. Well it would seem so, apart from the station, which had a loading area for the fishing industry, and a small harbour that did not exist in their time. In 2009, they knew that looking from Robin Hood's Bay toward Raven-Scar all that could be seen in anything like clarity, was the large Raven Hotel. But now, looking towards where they knew to be the Raven Hotel, they could see quite clearly the town of Raven-Scar.

    Not only the town could be seen, but how large the harbour was at the foot of the cliffs: it was a good size, with a stretch of sand that ran around under the cliffs. They decided that they had to explore the town of Raven-Scar when the opportunity arose. The incline lift that could be seen, looked very much like the ones they knew of at Scarborough. They just had to use that.

    Their time at Robin Hood's Bay passed quite pleasantly and quickly. As they climbed back up the steep main street to the charabanc stop, they heard the train whistle blowing as the engine puffed up the incline to Robin Hood's Bay. They were just in time to catch the last charabanc back to Raven-Scar, in time to listen to Cyril speaking to Sergeant Fellows.

    'Yes hello, I want to speak to Sergeant Fellows this is PC Whitaker from Raven-Scar, thank you'. There was a pause as Cyril listened to the ear piece. 'Hello is that Sergeant Fellows, ah! this is PC Whittaker from Raven-Scar. Sergeant, this is a funny sort of question, but can you tell me if you have any report of two children missing from an asylum,,, well anywhere in the vicinity,,, yes I've heard of Green Lane,,, no you haven't? No, no it's just, well I have a little problem but I think I can clear it up. Pardon! my goodness where,,, I see do you need any help from me?,,, right thank you sergeant,,, no I can handle this here. Call

Raven-Scar or the town that never was

me if you need any assistance.' Replacing the receiver he turned to the others with a strange expression on his face.

'Cyril is there anything wrong?' asked Agnes.

'Erm, not with anything to do with escaped asylum inmates, but the Sergeant has a peculiar happening. He thinks that a member of the public has committed suicide on the railway, but. And this is the weird part, he says that the person is dressed very strangely and has unusual things on his person. He described something very similar to what Harry calls his mobile. The body has been taken to the morgue in Whitby, to be examined.'

'Good lord, Cyril if another person like these two is here what on earth is happening. Just a minute, do you remember last year with that robbery at Marlow's, the man was never found. Then Mr Marlow did say there was something very odd about his appearance.'

Agnes was beginning to doubt her doubts; could it be true what Harry and Tina was saying? She still was not fully convinced.

'Yes I do remember that, just a moment let me look at the records, when was it dear?'

'November I think I know you were baffled by it.'

Cyril opened up a large filling cabinet; it was wooden, about three feet in width, with a roller door going all the way down to the floor ending in a locking clasp. He rummaged through his files and lifted out the one he was looking for; placing the file on the desk he opened it up, as the report covered four pages of hand written text, and was all in neat copper plate script. Cyril glanced through the pages until he came to the relevant paragraph.

'Listen to this. I made the investigation myself and even then I was puzzled. "The jewellers named Marlow, address, 10 Station Rd, Raven-Scar, suffered a daylight robbery at 9am on Friday the 17 November. Having a large display of quality jewellery, both in the window and in the counter, when asked why such a quantity, Mr Marlow explained that this was his Christmas stock and that he was expecting a large trade from Scarborough, as he was the only jeweller to stock precious stones and gold, being that he is a diamond trader. His explanation is as follows. 'I opened my door at 8-45 on the morning of the 17th. I noticed a large, dark-haired man, looking at my window display. I noticed his strange way of dress - a very bright yellow type of jacket, with a head covering like a hood, black trousers and white shoes. He looked at me and asked when I opened, I said 9a.m. I went back inside my shop behind the counter and the man followed me in and he asked to look at the most expensive gold and diamond rings on a tray. There were twenty rings on the tray, with a value of £300, the most expensive in the shop, He also asked to look at three diamond necklaces, value of £900. I did say this is my most busy time of year and why I have so much expensive stock.

The man looked at all of the display then putting a bag on the counter. I noticed it had a white tick on the bag. He stated that he had a gun in his pocket and would shoot me if I did not fill this bag with my display, then he hit me such a blow that I fell down and before I could recover he had dashed out the door and just seemed to vanish into the sea fret which was very heavy on that day. I gave PC Whitaker a full description of the assailant.'

'Now Harry and Tina, does that sound familiar to you, I mean the way the person was dressed?' Agnes started to speak but Cyril held up his hand; his wife, subdued, sat down.

'That's incredible Cyril, I mean if what this Mr Marlow says is true then I can explain what the man was wearing: the jacket is called 'a high vis garment' it's used by all sorts of workers from railway to builders. It sounds like he had a pair of trainers on; these are special shoes that most people wear. Although my dad never wears them, he says they are slovenly, and the bag with a white tick on it, which has to be a Nike bag, the tick is a logo. Sorry a logo is a manufactures sign, that this is an item made and sold by them. Tina this means that someone else has come from our time into this one. Cyril can we look at the man that they think has committed suicide?'

'Not tonight Harry, it's getting on for eleven o clock and I think it's time for us to get some sleep. In the morning I'll get in touch with Whitby and sort something out. Now Harry, if you don't mind you'll have to sleep in one of the cells again: it'll be cold I dare say but if we give you enough blankets you should be alright. Agnes dear have we got any of those ex-army blankets?'

Agnes said of course, she had made sure she bought plenty at the sale. Harry was given the eiderdown and three very hairy blankets that irritated his neck throughout the night, as he tossed and turned, his mind not quite grasping the strange situation both he and Tina found themselves in.

Tina flopped into the bed which Agnes made up for her. The mattress she found was very comfortable, with small feathers poking out of it along some of the seams, a large feather-filled eiderdown and the hot brick which she snuggled up to. Her last thought was for Harry in his cell, poor Harry.

Cyril had spent a lot of time on the telephone speaking to Sergeant fellows in Whitby. He told the Sergeant that Harry could help in identification of the clothing and items found in the person's rucksack, but, as Cyril went on, Harry could not identify the actual person. It took Cyril a lot of cajoling and a lot of explaining, to get permission from Sergeant Fellows, for Harry to look at the body.

Finally the Sergeant admitted that he needed help, as the items found mystified him. He agreed to send the Police van from Whitby to Raven-Scar to take Harry, Tina and Cyril to the Police Station in Whitby, where Harry would be shown the body that lay on the cold stone slab in the morgue.

CHAPTER 9

Now the three of them, at ten-thirty in the morning, stood speaking to Sergeant Fellows in the outer office of Whitby Police Station. Sergeant Fellows was speaking to his Constable.

As Sergeant Fellows was talking he was walking towards the Police Station door. Opening it, he beckoned for the three of them to follow him, as he strode away, still talking to Cyril.

'I'm still not too sure about this Cyril; it's highly irregular for a lad as young as Harry to look at anything like this. Still if he thinks he knows this person, then for this once I'll bend the rules. By the way, what's the lad's name, Harry what?'

'Mortimer. Sergeant, let me tell you this lad is different, very different. I don't think he can identify this person, but he knows all about the things you have found so strange.'

'Different, I don't understand Constable; different to what? I must say you are being rather vague and evasive about this lad. All right come on, the body is in the morgue. By the way you know the robbery that took place on your patch last year, you know, the jeweller? Well something just as weird happened three days ago in Guisborough; the coppers up there are going barmy trying to make sense of it.'

'I haven't heard of a jewellery robbery in Guisborough?' Cyril replied.

'No now I think about it you wouldn't have, not yet anyway and it wasn't a jeweller, it was the Middlesbrough Bank: there was a peculiar aspect to it. The funny thing about it was that the chap didn't take money, he wanted the gold coins that had been put in a safe deposit box by the mine owner and not only coins but gold bullion. How he

Raven-Scar or the town that never was

knew about the gold I don't know? But he just threatened with a shotgun and asked for the gold: just like that, it fair shook up the staff I can tell you. Then the alarm was raised and he rode off on a motor bicycle; a funny one at that according to an eye-witness. He rode to the rail station, then when the lads got there, no-one had seen hide nor hair of the chap. He just vanished, poof like that. My feeling, for what it's worth, is that he made his was across country, but I wouldn't think it possible on a motor bicycle, would you? It's a bit rough at the top of Guisborough, then ont' moors but it's the only place 'e could have gone. Still any road, the mine owner has put up a substantial reward for information £500, by 'eck what I could do wi' that amount of brass. Between you and me Constable, I don't think we'll find this bank-robber somehow? Ah, here we are the county morgue, are you sure you want to see the cadaver young man?'

Harry said yes, but Tina shook her head saying that she did not think it would be good for her to see this person as she felt sick at the idea. Harry was undaunted and followed the Sergeant and Cyril down the stone steps into the morgue which, to keep it cold so that the bodies did not decay too quickly, was built below ground level. Harry shivered, not from fright, but from the cold, clammy atmosphere. A strong smell of disinfectant hung in the air.

Harry wanted to study medicine, if he ever got back to his own time; he also had thought about archaeology, so to see a dead person was not too disruptive. The body lay on a marble slab covered by a white cloth, the attendant uncovered the face. The head looked perfectly normal, it was below the neck where the train had hit the man and caused severe damage to his lower limbs, Harry was not shown that. The attendant spoke to Harry.

'Do you recognise this man?' he asked.

'Well hardly, there must be thousands of people walking along the rail track. It used to be called the Lyke Wake Walk and went over the moors from coast to coast,' Harry was cut short in his explanation.

'I have no idea what you are referring to young man, nobody walks on the railway. I mean nobody deliberately walks on it like this chap did, and whatever is this Lake Walk you talk about? All we want to know is do you recognise this person?'

'No definitely not.'

'Right thank you; at least we have a name, taken from a wallet. Mr Fellows has that, along with some very unusual items. Oh! yes, just one moment, take a look at his clothing please? You may throw some light on those.'

The attendant took Harry and Cyril into another room where on a table was a pile of clothing, Harry looked at the labels; the clothing was obviously from his and Tina's time. The waterproof jacket was a lined Gore-Tex one, the trousers labelled Rohan, and the boots had the name Chris Brasher Fell Boots on the tag. Harry said he would like to speak to the two Constables privately. They followed the morgue attendant back up the stairs, Sergeant Fellows signed the register, stating that the body had been inspected by him and the Constable. He did not mention Harry. They left the morgue and went back to the police station: all four then went into a room, which was the Sergeants office; a small fire burned in the fire grate making the room slightly warmer than the outer office.

As the four of them sat for a few moments in silence, they gathered their thoughts, the small fire spat and crackled. Finally Sergeant Fellows spoke

'Well Harry lad anything unusual? I must say the clothing is very well made and the jacket is more like the Lifeboat Service would wear, a bit like an oilskin, and those boots I wouldn't mind some like those meself like? Carry on lad 'owt else? Ah hang on, this is what we found on yon chap in this shoulder bag,' Sergeant Fellows, placed items he took out of the bag and put them on the table. 'Right lad, tell me what these are because they look very unusual to me?' Harry and Tina looked through the belongings of the dead person, his driving licence carried the name of John Broadbent, of 122 Harehills Lane, Leeds.

'So what's that?' asked Cyril.

'It's a driving licence to drive a car.'

'Car what car, do you mean an automobile?'

'Yes.'

'You said it was a licence, why do you need a licence to drive an automobile?'

'In our time Sergeant you had to take a driving test, if you passed it, then it entitled you to drive a car.' The Sergeant had missed what Harry had said 'in our time' he would come back to that later.

'An automobile you mean?'

'Yes only the term automobile changed to the cars to be called motor cars, but we just call them cars.'

'You mean he can drive an automobile, now that's very interesting, we don't have many of those round here, certainly not in Whitby. I think the lord Mayor has one and Dr Davis; blimey he must be a rich person to afford one of those new-fangled things. I have to say I don't reckon much to them, the noise scares horses, and people, and they go too fast for their own good I say. Still if yon bloke comes from Leeds, there must be a lot of money in Leeds, I suppose with all the mills and engineering.' Sergeant Fellows made his point that cars were doomed, horses were much better.

CHAPTER 10

'And this is a mobile phone' Harry switched the phone on it had enough charge to light up he passed it to the Sergeant, 'press that button?'

'Oh my lord, what on earth is this?' the Sergeant nearly dropped the phone as the screen lit up and bleeped; the command from it stated that no signal was available.

'Press that button and don't drop it'

'It's, erm, telling me that I can play worms or something.'

The Sergeant was holding a piece of technology not yet invented in his time or world. Because by now it was became clearer to Harry and Tina, that not only had they gone back in time, but somehow they had shifted in time to a near parallel world. How or why this had happened, they could not explain. So that now with the discovery of poor Mr Broadbent and the knowledge of a 'bank robber', it was obvious that somewhere along the old Scarborough to Whitby rail line, at certain times, a curtain was opened allowing access to this world of 1909. It needed a scientist to explain this phenomena, as of now the contents of a rucksack were displayed on the table. The contents from a 2009 bag resided on a table 100 years in the past, in an alternate world at that. No wonder Harry and Tina were confused and apprehensive. The second object was a pair of binoculars, then a thermos flask plus a plastic box with a banana in it Mr Broadbent's snack, a compass, and a map.

'Just a minute young man what the devil is this thing I've got 'old of?' The Sergeant still held Mr Broadbent's phone.

'It's a telephone' said Tina.

Raven-Scar or the town that never was

'Now don't get saucy with me young lady this is not a telephone, some sort of magic lantern perhaps but a telephone it is not.'

The Sergeant was in no mood for silly games and if this nonsense went on any further he would not only lose his temper he would have no compunction but to lock these two cheeky youngsters in his cells. Pointing across the room to the telephone standing upright on his desk, he stated that was a telephone. Harry and Tina agreed with him, and then looking at Cyril for guidance the Constable shrugged his shoulders and turned to the Sergeant.

'I think it would be better if we took all this stuff into the interview room Sergeant. The two young persons will tell you where they came from and the mysterious way in which they came 'ere.' Sometimes Cyril slipped into the local dialect of North Yorkshire: the items were collected up and into the interview room the four of them trooped.

The room was cold and bare, four chairs and a wooden table sat in the middle; iron bars told that this was a police cell and when the door was locked there would be no way out. Piling the rucksack and objects on the table, they sat down, but not before Cyril suggested that a mug of tea might be appropriate. The Sergeant, called one of his Constables to kindly provide tea and a few biscuits for them; the beverage arrived and the biscuits were consumed by Harry and Tina.

'Right now what is it I am supposed to hear, and none of your lying like you did with that so called telephone?' Sergeant Fellows did not take kindly to people lying to him, he could spot a liar a mile off. 'Right lad you first'; but before Harry could speak Cyril interrupted him.

'I think I should tell you what I know first Sergeant. These two suddenly appeared at the café in Raven-Scar. They asked for two glasses of coke,' the Sergeant was about to interrupt. 'Yes bear with me please Sergeant, and then they wanted to pay with coins, these coins actually.' Cyril took the money out of his pocket. 'They also had paper money to the amount of £10 with the head of a Queen on them.' Again the Sergeant was going to interrupt. 'Wait please Sergeant all in good time. They both said they had ridden their bikes from Scarborough up the 'old rail line' their exact words. They were dressed in a similar clothing to the deceased, both dressed in shorts as if they were taking part in some form of sprinting. The young lady was, when I first saw her, dressed very unseemly, but that can be explained.' Cyril took a deep breath and continued. 'Now I inspected the coins and the paper money, have a close look Sergeant and tell me in your experience what you make of them; here take this five pound note. The bicycles I also had a very close look at and I can quite honestly say I have never seen any like them, and I have no doubt you will say the same. Now I'll let these two take over, but Sergeant, listen to what they say 'afore you say anything.' Before Harry could speak Tina interrupted him.

'Harry please, show them the map? Lay it out on the table and let them see it properly.'

'Good idea, shift some of this stuff off the table please then I can spread the map out.'

Soon a space was made and Harry with Tina's help spread the Ordnance Survey map out it was by no means a new map the date on it was 1997, but it was more than relevant to their aims of trying to explain their situation and of course it was printed on paper, whereas a hundred years ago the map would have been printed on linen. Tina smoothed it out and held one corner whilst the two policemen scanned the map.

'Now then you two this is not a proper map. For some reason you are trying to mislead PC Whitaker and myself; why I shall find out? This map is definitely wrong or a very old one because it does not show neither the railway or, and more important, it definitely does not show Raven-Scar: well it does but not the town. Next thing I suppose is that you will say that Raven-Scar never was. Ha ha a likely story that is and no mistake.'

Raven-Scar or the town that never was

'That's just it Sergeant it doesn't exist, well not in our time anyway, it never did. I can tell you that in our time it was proposed that a town called Ravenscar would have been built, I mean plots of land were purchased and drains and streets were built. It was going to be a resort in between Whitby and Scarborough, but either money ran out or the original investors found that people would not go there because it would be unsuitable. It did not have a beach. And another thing, it would be very difficult to build a harbour. Although it may seem strange talking to you now, a railway station was built, and that's another thing the railway did exist, it ran from Scarborough through Staintondale and Robin Hoods bay to Whitby; then even that was taken away in 1965 I think.'

'Just one minute young man, do you think I have lost my reason? You are saying to me that you do not come from here and you do not believe either the railway or Raven-scar exist. Well it obviously does or PC Whitaker is in charge of something that isn't there. Come on now we all like a joke, but this is going too far. Look as far as I am concerned, I can overlook one or two lies, but you are telling me things that I know are most certainly untrue.' Holding up his hand before Tina or Harry could object. 'All right I have listened to your explanations but I cannot in all honesty believe you're ranting on about things that have no substance, so, and for now, I shall have to commit you to the cells for further investigation.'

'No, no listen to us please we are telling the truth honestly we are; look at the map, look at our money can you see the dates on them?' Tina was beginning to despair with this Sergeant; how had he become so important if he discredited everything that was said to him.

'The date on this map says 1997 that's obviously a misprint and I must say the map is not a good one in fact I have never seen a map printed on paper. Maps are on linen, they have to be. For a start most maps are for the use of the Army or the Royal Navy, and the maps I have are very accurate. This map does not show anything that should be here, so in my opinion it is a fake and you two are some sort of con-men, or con-girl if there is such a thing.'

'Take a look at our money, hold the note up to the light can you see the watermark?' The Sergeant nodded. 'See that proves it's real money and our coins: look this is a one pound coin look at the inscription and the writing on the sides; the pound coin might look like a sovereign but in our time it is only worth one pound, and the other coins are what is stamped on the surface would any forger go to such lengths as that just to produce fake coins?' Harry had a very good point there; good fakes were just that, good, but there was always a flaw somewhere.

On careful examination of the money which Tina and Harry placed on the table, the Sergeant was somewhat perplexed. He stood up and looked more closely at the map tracing his finger over the route of the railway and roads, following them right to the end of the printing where the map would show the route and where the next town or village was.

He looked at Guisborough, Great Ayton and followed his finger to Stokesley back through Helmsley then Malton looking at where York was shown then following his digit back to Scarborough, all the while shaking his head in disbelief. Looking at Cyril he asked his opinion.

CHAPTER 11

'I know this sounds very far-fetched Sergeant, but I believe that Harry and Tina are from another time, and possibly another world. By that I mean one similar to ours but different, as if there were two parallel star systems. I've read the theory but I must confess it does sound unlikely as we understand things, but if what these two say is true then the theory exists. Just think of what the scientists will make of this?'

'The theory does exist'. Tina broke into the conversation. 'It is envisaged in Einstein's theory of relativity, $E=MC2$, that's the equation we are doing physics at school and I remember that, the theory shows that there should be a fourth dimension, I think?' Tina was becoming out of her depth she looked cross at Harry who just shrugged his shoulders as if to say "carry on you are doing well." So Tina did carry on, 'and I think what Cyril said about a 'curtain' in time must be true, and that means we have to find that 'curtain' for us to return back to our time. It must have something to do with the old railway.'

She stopped talking as Cyril interjected.

'I know it may sound farfetched but that could explain a) the Robberies b) this person Broadbent and one or two other oddities.'

'You mean this chap stepped in front of a train deliberately?' queried the Sergeant.

'No not deliberately, if he came from the same time as Harry and Tina he would not expect a train at all. They have said that the railway no longer exists in their time: don't you see he wasn't expecting a train, he must have gone through this so called 'curtain' just as the train was on it's way and it killed him now that, if I may say so is very, very unfortunate. I mean stepping through time and finding a train where one is not supposed to be is very unfortunate indeed.'

Sergeant Fellows sighed, it sounded as if the world's troubles lay on his shoulders. 'And there was something else we found in this Mr Broadbent's haversack, small thing quite heavy, about the size of a packet of fags.'

'Fags?' queried Tina.

'Aye, fags, cigarettes then, about that size,' he demonstrated holding his thumb and forefinger about ten centre metres apart. 'With buttons and a little black window in the back, we tried to make sense 'on it but now't worked, maybe lad you can 'ave a look, that is if it 'asn't gone on train, come on lets 'ave a word with PC Turnbull'.

The Police Station at Whitby was considerably larger than the one at Raven-Scar. Entering the outer office, the Sergeant called out.

'David 'ave we still got that parcel we were sending to York or has it gone on train?'

'No, still here Sarge I'm just going down to the station to put it on the 6 o-clock one to Scarborough; its here on top of the counter, why do you want to have another look?'

'Not me lad: this young feller 'ere would like a look at it pass it over please?'

The parcel was handed over and the Sergeant slit open the paper parcel with a knife, handing the item to Harry, who knew immediately that it was a digital camera. An Olympus, he pressed the START button and the camera came to life, the lens slid smoothly out. Harry pointed the camera at the three Policemen standing against the counter. The room was not as bright as it could have been so the 'Flash ready' sign blinked on; Harry pressed the 'go' button and the room lit up for a fraction of a second, temporally blinding the three PCs.

Raven-Scar or the town that never was

'What the 'ell did you do that for? What did you do? Give that thing to me?' The Sergeant made a grab for the camera but Harry held on to it.

'No Sergeant, I want you to look at this little screen on the back, this is a camera and the black window you mentioned is a screen, a bit like a cinema screen'. Blank faces stared at him. 'Oh! no cinema,' three heads shook from side to side slowly. Harry stood in the middle of the group, Tina stood to one side with a grin on her face she knew what was coming. Harry lifted up the camera holding the back of it so that they could see the small screen, as he pressed the 'on' button the screen lit up, scrolling through the pictures he stopped at the one he wanted.

'Nay lad what the 'eck, is that us lot there? I don't understand how you did that but it's a damn good trick right fair it is.' Cyril was stumped for anything else to say as they looked at the three Policemen looking slightly startled as the flash went off.

'It's not a trick Cyril this is a camera, like nothing you have seen of nor heard of, this is technology 100 years from now, it's called digital because it stores all the pictures on a memory chip, this camera can take, let me see.' Harry looked at the top edge of the tiny screen he saw the figure 300. '300 photos that's how many this little camera can take.' Handing the camera to Cyril he showed him how to forward and reverse the images. Cyril nearly dropped the camera in his excitement, as the images scrolled forward, some showed the view from the cliff tops out to sea, one image had captured a huge container ship heading north, another showed the orange coloured RNLI boat ploughing through the waves, another image was of three Victorian houses standing on their own with, as a backdrop, a long concrete platform.

'Hold that one Cyril look at it very closely does it remind you of somewhere, somewhere that you are very familiar with?' asked Harry.

Cyril gazed at the small but clear image of three houses and the extinct rail-way platform, with trees and shrubs growing around it, the 'turning circle' that Tina and Harry had recently walked on as they entered the café. As the PC studied the picture for a few moments he puffed out his cheeks so then he passed the camera over to the Sergeant and PC Turnbull, both shook their heads. Cyril licked his dry lips and started to speak but his mouth was very dry, this was beyond anything that he knew of.

'I erm, think it's the café and the station back home.'

'What don't be daft man that's now't like Raven-Scar station and those 'ouse's 'ave a café just where that one is' the Sergeant pointed at the picture, as he took the camera from Cyril's hand. 'Well I'm blessed,' as he saw the café in the photo. Turning to the constable he pointed to the desk that stood adjacent to the front door of the Station House, members of the public would be attended to at this desk. 'Constable look after the front desk please? I'm taking these three into my office.'

Raven-Scar or the town that never was

CHAPTER 12

The station office was large enough for four people to sit on chairs that stood against a wall: the Sergeant seated himself behind a dark wooden desk; he lit up a pipe, and as the aromatic smoke curled upwards, he rested his elbows on the desk top looking at Harry and Tina with a searching gaze. He puffed away until his pipe resembled a small steam train: speaking through clenched teeth not removing his pipe he addressed Cyril first.

'PC Whitaker can you explain to me what is going on, something very strange is happening in this neighbourhood; first we 'ave two robberies that are surrounded in mystery. Then two young people suddenly turn up with 'funny' money which they claim is genuine, and it carries a Queen's head. Not just a Queen but one called Elizabeth. If my history is correct, Elizabeth died in the 14th cent or thereabouts. No don't interrupt me constable, let me finish; then two engine drivers claim that a man they killed appeared from nowhere, not only that but he had some very peculiar items on his person, including this item which you two,' pointing at Harry and Tina. 'Claim to be a camera. Now for your information, we happen to have a camera in this police station, which we use to photograph the scene of a crime and it is nothing like that little thing there. So questions, first who are you? And where are you from? Second you said in the other room that that thing is, what did you say? Aha yes technology, which you said was 100 years ahead in time. Now you two listen to me I am not like PC Whitaker, I can be very awkward and obstinate. You have spun some yarn to PC Whitaker about not being of this world or time; now you and I know that, that, is total nonsense.' The Sergeant had lost a lot of his Yorkshire dialect he was in interrogating mode. 'Next you will be telling us that man is on the moon.'

'Yes' said Tina.

'Pardon young lady what did you say?'

'I said yes there have been men on the moon quite a lot in fact also space ships are reaching beyond the galaxy. There has been a satellite landing on Mars and satellites have photographed Mercury and Saturn. We have aeroplanes that fly faster than sound and motor cars that can exceed 100 miles an hour.'

'Stop there madam that is utter nonsense.' The Sergeant was losing his temper and had started to raise his voice. 'If man travelled at that speed he would die, the fastest man has been so far is! What am I saying, you are talking absolute nonsense, so let us have a proper discussion without your imagination running away with you.'

Meanwhile Harry was scrolling through the camera's images there were a few taken at a motor-cycle race, more of cars, and he counted eight taken at the rail museum in York.

'Sergeant can I interrupt you for a moment, take a look at these?' Harry came round the edge of the desk and placed the camera on the flat surface, the image was bright due to the office being lit by one electric bulb, so the trains showed up very clearly. The first image was of an engine from 1878, tall chimney, huge driving wheels and an open cab. The second showed a more enclosed engine about the same year as they were in 1909. The Sergeant sucked his breath in as he looked at the images scrolling before his eyes. The Mallard showed on the next but one frame. Then the last was the Japanese Bullet train which stands in the museum. The previous frame was the Rocket. The Sergeant's eyes nearly popped out of his head, he spluttered out his words.

Raven-Scar or the town that never was

'It's just a trick, a trick, those are models' he said for want of something that he could relate to.

'No they are real trains; look at the people standing near them. See how they are dressed, that's how we dress when not riding our bikes, and what we are wearing now.' Agnes Whitaker had been to the 'jumble sale' and Tina and Harry were now dressed in Edwardian clothes. 'are only seen in a museum; what we are telling you Sergeant, is the truth. We are from another time and as far as we can tell another world, how, we have no idea all we know is what we have explained repeatedly to you and PC Whitaker.' Harry drew in a deep breath. ' Which is, that just six days ago Tina and I went for a bike ride on the abandoned rail line that used to run, at least it did in our grandparents' time, from Scarborough to Whitby, and beyond I'm pretty certain it went through Sandsend up to Redcar. Anyway we are just as mystified as you. And we want to find a way back to our time, all we can say for definite is that as we approached the old station at Raven-Scar we went through some very cold rather dense fog, and then we found ourselves here in your time. Nothing mysterious happened to us like falling through a 'black hole' or anything like that we just sort of popped out into your time, and that can also explain how the poor man whose camera we are looking at collided with the train. If he came from our time which it looks like, he would not expect anything on that line least of all a train. Sorry if we don't make a lot of sense but we can't make sense of it ourselves. PC Whitaker and his wife have let us stay in their house, although I still sleep in a cell, but they have been very kind to us and I think that Cyril does in some way believe our story as I say we are sorry for all this confusion.'

As Harry finished his explanation the telephone rang.

'Hello Sergeant Fellowes speaking, yes that's correct we were over there when the robbery had taken place,,,, pardon can you repeat that the line is very bad,,,,, thick fog you say oh, I see, ,,pardon say that again,,, where at the Yorkshire Bank here in Whitby? Right Constable I'll be right over'.

Replacing the phone, he looked at the group in the room. 'There has been a shooting at the Yorkshire and it sounds like the bank manager has been shot and is in hospital, very serious the constable said, and this time the man escaped on a motor vehicle of some kind, a two wheeled one with an engine in it. The PC said it looked like one of those new things you know a motor-bicycle, but he did say it looked very weird to him.'

'Well it would, wouldn't it if he came from our time, he would have ridden along the rail track and come out in Whitby, and he must have been riding a trail bike.'

'A what bike?' asked Cyril.

'A trail bike one that goes off road: in our time motor-cycles are very popular and I have to say that our roads are far better then what you have, most of your roads are cobbles, well they are in Raven-Scar at least, and a special type of motor-bicycle is made that can travel over very rough ground. I don't know about you but I think it's a great possibility that this man has found a way to leave his own time or ours if you prefer, and he's even found how to return. If we can catch him then we have the chance to return also, I hope.' Harry said this without much conviction.

Tina's phone gave a brrr, the battery was running down, and she asked Harry if his phone still had enough battery power left, the answer was yes but not very much.

Meantime Sergeant Fellows had instructed PC Whitaker to contact the Cavalry barracks in Scarborough, to call out armed men to search the surrounding area for the armed bank robber,

'If you don't mind me saying Sergeant that would be a waste of time if as Harry thinks that this person is doing what it looks like he is doing then don't you think he would have returned back into our time? It's just a thought.' Tina was correct; the gunman would do precisely that.

Raven-Scar or the town that never was

'You're probably right but a man has been seriously injured and may die, so I have no choice but to call on all resources, and the army can send a truck load of soldiers in a couple of hours from Scarborough, Constable have you contacted them yet?'

'Yes Sergeant, they are on their way, what now?'

'Now we get into the police van and, get down to the bank. I think it advisable that you two youngsters come along with us, your story is unbelievable I have to say, but, well I don't know. Somehow I am coming round to accepting it if only for the reason that I have no option.' On the way down to the Bank in the centre of town the Sergeant asked a question.

'Harry have you any idea why this person only asks for and takes gold coins or bullion? Not that we get much of those but the Yorkshire is a clearing bank so I suppose it does have a certain amount of gold in the safe. But why not money I mean there must be oh! £10-15,000 in the safe at any time and that is worth taking it's a fortune.'

'No think about it for a minute, this money is 1909 it would have no value 100 years from now would it, well it would I suppose to a collector. But he would not be able to spend one pence of it,' he grinned when he said that. 'Or in your words a penny of it; no Sergeant gold is a much better option for him, even a relatively small amount is worth robbing for.'

'He's right Sergeant I've looked closely at the money these two have and I think it's genuine. Whether anyone says their story is poppycock or not their story, that money, and their bikes are genuine I'm convinced of it.' Cyril was now 99% certain that Harry and Tina were what they say they are.

CHAPTER 13

In the back of the Police van Harry and Tina were being rattled and shaken about, the van had very little springing in its suspension and the solid rubber tyres made for an uncomfortable ride in the back. The van pulled up outside of the bank, where the Sergeant was given the news that the bank manager had died.

'Now it's murder, did we get a good description of the villain?'

'Not really Sergeant but what we did get was that the person was dressed very similar to the person that robbed both the bank in Guisborough and Marlow's in Raven-Scar. Only this time he deliberately rode onto the railway, and that's the last anybody saw or heard him. There's something very fishy about all this Sergeant, any idea what it's all about?'

'If I told you Constable you just would not believe me. 'Phone the local magistrate and tell him I've called out the army to make a search over the moors and roads.'

'Right Sergeant,' PC Turnbull strode into the bank and asked to use the phone, raising the mouthpiece to his lips he jiggled the speaker cradle up and down. 'Is that the operator? This is PC Turnbull connect me to Mr Bellamy the Magistrate, quickly this is police business.' He waited a while until Mr Bellamy came to the phone. ' Mr Bellamy this is PC Turnbull I'm speaking from the Yorkshire bank, can you come down here please,,,, yes it is urgent, a robbery has been committed and a more serious assault has been carried out on the bank manager,,, yes very serious, pardon? how serious well he's been shot, yes shot,, pardon,, yes he was taken to the hospital,,, yes I said. We have just learnt that he has unfortunately died,,,, mmm, yes about an hour ago,,,, I don't know why you weren't told we have been a bit busy,,,, half an hour you say thank you sir we will still be here we have things to do. The Sergeant has called out the army to organise a search, both on the moors and surrounding villages,,, hard to say sir the man seems to have vanished,,,, thank you sir.'

The Constable reported back to his Sergeant that the Magistrate was on his way and would be there in 30 minutes.

The bank had closed its doors, a crowd had gathered on the pavement,

'Get rid of this lot Constable for goodness sake there's n'owt they can do.'

Entering the bank the Sergeant, Cyril, Harry and Tina were confronted by frightened staff all crowding behind the tellers counter; the Sergeant took control.

'Right now let me have as good a description as you can give me. Who's in charge now?' A small man dressed in black waistcoat, jacket and pin striped trousers stepped forward. 'Ah! right can I have your name sir please? Take this down Constable?' Cyril had his note book out and licked the point of his pencil.

'My name is Smith, Wilfred Smith Sergeant, I am the chief teller. I must say we are all very shaken up by all of this, poor Mr Latimer. The man took him into his own office, you know and made him open the main safe, and then he asked Mr Latimer for all the gold coins and bullion. We had quite a substantial amount in at the time, mainly sovereigns of course, exactly five thousand pounds to be exact. The amount of bullion was more of course but that is something I can't at this moment tell you? Mr Latimer tried to stop the man, he grappled with the gun and it went off. Mr Latimer fell down; we knew he had been hurt.'

'Are you telling me that the robber did not intentionally shoot Mr Latimer?'

'Yes I am Sergeant I don't think it was intentional, nonetheless a murder has been committed has it not?'

'It has indeed Mr Smith that is why I need all the details from you; my Constable will interview the other witnesses.

How many shots did you hear?' Mr Smith replied that he heard only one shot. ' Now how heavy was the bullion? Was it very heavy I mean could a man lift it, as far as I am aware bullion comes in ingots and weighs a lot.'

At that precise moment one of the bank clerks came up to Mr Smith and said something in a quiet voice. Mr Smith said 'Thank you very much John.'

'There were four ingots, John has told me, all of course are gone. Each ingot weighs 25 lbs. But he was a big man Sergeant and he lifted the bag easily. I didn't see him ride off but we heard the sound of the engine and then it stopped, we thought he had been stopped, but the people that did notice him said he rode towards the station. Then, I know this sounds most odd, but he rode towards Scarborough, he must have come through Raven-Scar?'

'Did you hear the motor-cycle after that?'

'Now you mention it Sergeant, no we didn't, it stopped suddenly. Oh! Another thing and I think you will find this very important, he dropped the gun; Miss Handley picked it up. I did tell her to be careful as it may have fingerprints on it. I take it you can take fingerprints Sergeant?'

'Yes we do have a fingerprint outfit at the station, very fortunate for us that we have, this new system was only approved by Parliament only last month. Is this the weapon?'

Sergeant Fellows was handed the shotgun he noticed the gun had been cut down so as to make it easier to carry as a full size shotgun is nearly four feet in length. Now it was a more manageable twenty four inches. The Sergeant handled the gun with his handkerchief, aware that if there were any fingerprints, then his own would not be shown when the fingerprinting expert applied powder to the weapon. A puzzled expression came over the face of the Sergeant he was examining the shortened gun closely turning to PC Whitaker he asked for his opinion. Cyril took the gun, looking at the Sergeant, then at Harry.

Raven-Scar or the town that never was

'See 'owt peculiar with this gun Harry lad?' Harry took the gun inspecting it closely.

'No Cyril nothing strange it's been cut down of course I think that's what bank robbers do with shotguns, why do you ask?'

'The barrels lad, look at the barrel.'

'Yes what's wrong with them?'

'Wrong!, Harry they are upside down shotgun barrels are side by side, not upside down, and the hammers where are the hammers?'

Harry knew very little about shotguns, but he knew enough to move the 'locking' lever on the top back-strap of the shotgun to 'break' open the weapon exposing the firing pins inside. Which is precisely what he did.

'The firing pins are inside here look, I think this gun is called an 'over under' I don't know much really but when I watched the Olympics this is the sort of gun they use. Look if I push this lever on the top the barrels drop open and the cartridges spring out. Can I have those spent cartridges Sergeant please? Now if I pop these into the barrel breach, close the gun, move this lever which has to be the safety catch, pull the trigger like so, BANG, then push this lever and look the cartridges are forced out by this mechanism.'

The empty cartridges flew out and clattered onto the tiled floor of the bank, the two policemen looked at each other. The Sergeant took the gun from Harry,

'I want the fire arms expert to have a look at this. Now Constable I want you to take these two young 'uns back to Raven-Scar, keep your eye on them because I want to speak to them later in the week. Let me see it's Tuesday to-day so say Friday, yes Friday constable I'll come over on the train and we can all discus what I think will be a very interesting meeting.'

The Sergeant did not know how interesting that meeting would be.

CHAPTER 14

Later when Cyril, Harry and Tina returned to Raven-Scar, and after they had, had a very respectable meal in the police Station house, few words were spoken about the day's events. Agnes wanted to know all about the 'murder' of which Cyril said 'Later love I'll tell you later.' Harry and Tina went off to their respective rooms, Harry to his 'Cell' and Tina to her cold bedroom with a hot brick wrapped in a towel for comfort. Before they parted Tina spoke to Harry.

'Harry all that's happening now, can this mean we have a chance to get out of this bizarre situation and somehow find out where and how this robber can easily come and go. He must have found something like a permanent portal or something don't you think?'

'You may be right, but until he does come back, and we have to hope he does, we have no way of finding out anything.'

'Harry, seriously do you think we can return to our time? Or will we remain here in 1909?' Tina shivered at the thought. 'I try not to think too much but what if we can't, our parents must be out of their minds wondering what on earth happened to us. I counted the days that we have been like this. Harry it's nearly three weeks, people will think we are dead. Oh heck I don't really want to think too much about it.'

Harry did not have an answer all he could do was kiss Tina on the cheek, give her a hug and say 'good night see you in the morning.' What else could he do? Tina looked to him for support and comfort, which he was more than happy to do. If he had wanted an adventure then his companion would have been Tina.

Friday morning and true to his word Sergeant Fellows appeared at eleven o clock; bringing with him another

Raven-Scar or the town that never was

person who reminded Tina of Sherlock Holmes. He wore a cape and Deer-Stalker hat and she expected him to pull out a curly pipe like Holmes. Instead this man, on sitting down, pulled out a packet of cigarettes and started puffing away.

The Police Station House room became fogged up with the smoke, all three Policemen smoked. Tina soon realized that smoking in this time was totally accepted; it seemed to her that apart from alcohol, cigarettes were the way that the poorer people in society, passed away a great deal of spare time.

Raven-Scar was a holiday resort and so most of the smaller houses would be owned by business men and rented out to workers in the holiday industry. She recalled that in the 17-18 Century, an Alum Mine was built on the cliff top, not far from her own Ravenscar. Naturally, she assumed that in this world, that would have employed a great number of labourers. If! That is there was a mine on these cliff tops. Then, unlike in her time, business had seen the potential of the railway; the Victorians were nothing if not ingenious, so hence Raven-Scar was built as a permanent place.

To put her mind at rest she had asked Cyril if a mine of any sort was built on Raven-Scar cliffs. Cyril had said to her that if she looked towards the edge of the town looking South East, she would see the top of a tall chimney. That was where the mine was, Alum mine? He thought so.

She and Harry had explored the town right down to the harbour. Down there stretching into the North Sea was a long pier with amusements and a theatre at the very end. Unlike the one that once graced Scarborough, but had been swept away in a storm, this one was solid. It even had a small train running along its length. She and Harry had walked out to the very end of this pier. The harbour had fishing boats and a small steamer, sheltering in its two sweeping arms.

To Tina this place was somehow magical, a sort of fairy tale land, well that's how it seemed to her. Harry had even paid for the two of them to ride back up the steep cliff on the 'tram-way' this one was very different to the ones in Scarborough.

At the top of the 'incline', the base of the 'tram' was filled with water in a large tank underneath it, making it heavier than the 'tram' at the bottom of the incline. This heavier 'tram' would move down wards pulling the lighter 'tram' up to the top, and then the reverse filling and emptying would take place.

She knew all about the power of water, this 'incline' reminded her that reading of the history of Ironbridge in Shropshire, there was a mention there of a water powered 'incline' . Her reading matter was all encompassing; she liked this small holiday town and wondered seriously why in her world it had come to nothing.

The road down to the harbour and small beach took them past the large Raven Hotel through some streets. They walked down Norman Road, onto Saxon Road and would continue down the cliffs: she new that in her time this place was a golf course. How weird, just a simple slip in time and she and Harry had entered another dimension. Tina was beginning to believe Harry about his fourth dimension, although the physics escaped her somewhat. She made a mental note to study the Laws of Physics when she hopefully got back to 2009; somehow she just knew that she and Harry would return, when? Well that was the 64 million dollar question was it not?

Raven-Scar, in this time and world was hyphenated; it reminded Tina a little bit like Filey. Slightly larger, the main street was longer and had more shops than Filey but none of the names rang any bells though. There was nothing like those in her time, no Boots, or W H Smith no M&S, no Waterstones, there was a large store called Rowntrees; that name did ring a bell.

Tina and Harry had noticed when they caught the Charabanc previously, that there was a Charabanc service

Raven-Scar or the town that never was

through the town; one even climbed down the steep road to the harbour. When they were both down there near the harbour, they had wanted to play on the machines in the 'Penny Arcade'. Unfortunately coins from the year 2009 and another world probably would not be accepted. Shame really because the old machines looked more interesting than the glowing, bleeping, screeching mechanisms on the sea front at Scarborough.

Now she and Harry had a meeting with the two Policemen and the stranger. They sat opposite the three men. On the table spread out was most of the items from the rucksack of Mr Broadbent. Sergeant Fellows introduced the third person.

'This gentleman is Mr Woods a detective inspector from Leeds. Mr Woods has a great deal of experience in matters that require, shall we say, a different way of thinking; he is also an expert in the new form of criminal identification called 'fingerprinting'. He is also an expert in firearms, which is one of the reasons he is here. He finds that this shotgun is totally beyond his recognition. I have explained, as much as I can, what PC Whitaker has told me and what I seem to have understood from our conversation with you two in Whitby. Now if you don't mind I would like you to tell detective Woods what you have explained to PC Whitaker and me. Harry I want you to be as clear as possible on what you say, alright carry on. Tina, I would like you to interrupt Harry if you think it necessary? Good, continue please Harry.'

Before Harry could speak the detective rolled the shotgun out from its cover onto the table looking at Harry he leaned forward.

'Harry this gun is like nothing I have seen before, I believe you called it an 'over under'? I take it that, that is because the barrels are one on top of the other, am I correct?'

'Yes that's correct I don't really know much about those things, although I do have an air- rifle, but as I told the Police in Whitby I watched the Olympics on TV and those are the guns that are used in the shooting discipline. I think that the design is pretty much standard as my dad would say, you would have to ask him for more inform,,,. Sorry I forgot you can't ask him can you?' then as an afterthought he continued with. 'No more than you would not understand what a TV is or the Olympics,' then he asked. 'Do you have the Olympic Games?'

DI Wood answered Harry.

'Yes we do as a matter of fact, do you? But of course that is a rhetorical question is it not? I am not as gullible as my colleagues so do not try to divert my questions Harry. Now young man I shall ask you a simple enough question, please answer truthfully. Why can I not Harry, why can I not ask your father? If you come from Scarborough we can soon send a Constable to get him,' Tina smiled at this. 'Is there something amusing you young lady?'

'There certainly is you would have to go forward a hundred years to ask Harry's dad anything?'

'Harry please, answer my question.'

'Alright I will, you cannot contact him because he is in our future not yours, also there just happens to be a lack of signal for our mobile phones. You haven't invented satellites yet, anyway that would be no use because we are all mixed up in this time differential thing.'

'Ah! yes now let us not go down that road, I neither understand, nor do I want to understand, something of what you have told my colleagues; we will come to that in time,' Tina nearly burst out laughing at the Inspectors use of the word time. 'All I want you to do is please Harry tell me more about all the things that are on the table - money for a start. Before you do I must tell you that we looked very closely at your money and the few coins we found on Mr Broadbent are very similar, how is that? Did you know the man?'

Raven-Scar or the town that never was

'No I did not, but he must have come here the same way that Tina and I did, a sort of time warp.'

'Yes, yes we'll go into all that later. So you did not know Mr Broadbent? Alright we will let that go for now; now this item? You call this a telephone, which really Harry this is no more a telephone than the man in the moon.'

'That's right.'

'What is?'

'The man in the moon, or rather the men on the moon, in our time we have men who have been to the moon and back.'

He was interrupted by detective Inspector Woods.

'Harry I can have you arrested for not cooperating with the police, men on the moon that's absurd and you know it.'

Tina broke into the conversation.

'No Mr Woods it is not absurd. We have both repeatedly told the same story over and over again. We are not from here, we are from some future time, not exactly your future time, that seems to be not so, but we are from the future. Now how, we cannot explain how, but we have passed through time just like Mr Broadbent, and, we also think the bank robber. We have somehow stumbled on a tear in time that's how we can explain it; it does seem implausible we know but in the very near future a scientist called Einstein and one called Planck, will expound a theory on relativity. That will explain that it is possible that a fourth dimension does exist.' Tina even surprised herself at this explanation: Harry even applauded her saying 'Well done Tina I couldn't have said it better myself.'

Tina sat back in her chair, and waited for the detective to answer her.

Mr Woods sat back in his chair, an air of bemusement flickered across his face. He lit another cigarette, drawing the smoke deep into his lungs, he let it out slowly. The smoke drifted upwards joining the lingering fumes already there, he addressed Harry.

'I want you to prove what you say Harry. If this is a telephone then prove it!'

'Harry there must be enough power left to try the phones, listen what if I take mine into the next room and you ring my number, or better still you stay here and I'll go into the next room, it might work come on Harry at least try it?' Tina pleaded with Harry.

'It's no use Tina.'

'Why Harry at least give it a try.'

'No I told you it's no use, partly because the batteries must be drained by now, but more importantly we can't get a signal. Tina just think for a moment the signal comes from a satellite, think about it. When were satellites put into space I mean communication satellites?'

'I don't know when?'

'About the 1960s, so you see the problem.'

'Oh, flip I forgot about that, but we can try Harry please just for me, please' Harry could not say no to Tina. He walked out of the room, Tina switched on her phone the screen lit up but the battery logo showed very little charge was left, they waited for a few minutes, then Harry walked back into the room.

'Sorry everybody it can't work the technology is not here and it won't be for around fifty years or so, if at all.'

'Harry try Mr Broadbent's phone.'

'Tina it's no use.'

'Please Harry, please you never know look what happened to us, we know we are not from here but we have to try to convince these people, we have to try.' Harry looked into Tina's eyes he knew it was their only chance, he also knew that unless a miracle happened there was no chance any of the three phones would ring. He left the room once more, two minutes later he was back.

'I told you it was no use', at that moment Mr Broadbent's phone suddenly rang, Harry threw it onto the table as if it was red hot, Detective woods picked it up.

Raven-Scar or the town that never was

'Hello this is Detective Woods speaking, who is that, hello,,,, yes that is me,,, pardon,,,, no he cannot answer he is,,,,' the phone went dead. 'That was someone asking for Mr Broadbent. I don't understand this at all, I mean this is not a phone and unless one of you two is a ventriloquist then I fail to see how you can say that it is. I am waiting for your answer?'

'Harry quick there must be one of those strange fogs out there somewhere near at hand Harry see if our phones work?'

Harry nearly dropped his phone in his eagerness to dial Tina's number. Her phone gave its ring tone 'jingle bells' don't ask, she listened to Harry's voice and passed her phone to Detective Woods, Harry spoke.

'Can you hear me, I'll go out of the room, now can you hear me?'

'My stars I can hear the lad, Harry I can hear you my god this is incredible, come back in Harry quick, Harry,,,, gone, Harry has gone.'

Harry walked back into the room holding Mr Broadbent's phone, placing it on the table all three phones, showed some battery life but that was all.

Communication with Harry and Tina's world had been severed, but the fraction of time could just be enough to convince the three Policemen that their story was true, would they be vindicated? Tina was thinking, if only they could find out where that slip in time was, then there was a chance of she and Harry returning to their world of 2009. She whispered to herself, 'Please let it happen again' but fate was definitely against her, for no further activity came from the three mobile phones, her own phone now showed a depleted battery logo, her shoulders slumped, if only, but it was too late, the law of physics crashed out of time.

If she and Harry had not taken so many photos of this Raven-Scar, both phones would have had more charge in them, too late to think of that now she thought.

CHAPTER 15

Detective Woods stood up from the table, he pulled out a watch held on a chain, and his face gave nothing away; placing the watch back into his waistcoat pocket he stood up.

'I want to catch the next train to Whitby, I want to make a lot of enquiries, Mr Fellows would you join me please? We can discuss this matter on the train.'

'Do you believe us now Detective?' Tina wanted to know his thoughts.

'On what I have just seen and what you have told me, I cannot in all honesty say 100% that I believe you. Let me ask a few people I know and in the next few days I will talk to you again. I apologise for leaving so abruptly but what I have just seen and heard, I have to question the validity of. I may be able to do that, on the other hand I may not at all, it depends on the conversation I can have with a few people I know. Constable when is the next train due?' he asked Cyril.

'Erm, let me see, its 4-30 pm now so the next train is at 4-45, you've just enough time to catch it.'

The two Policemen left the Raven-Scar Police house in a hurry. Cyril showed his concern for the two young people.

'Listen if it's any consolation I believe your story. All the things on this table point to engineering that is beyond our capabilities.'

'It's not engineering Cyril it's technology, and believe us when we say that this will, if your time moves along the same path as ours, which it seems to be doing, apart from some differences like major wars and so forth...'

'Harry don't say any more please I would rather not know our future, even if it does differ from yours and Tina's, leave me with some thoughts on where my future lies, such as it is.'

Agnes bustled in.

'Look loves it's getting very late now so come on I've med some dinner so let's eat and we can talk at the same time.'

The four of them went into the kitchen now warm and cosy with the coal fire burning brightly. Four places were laid at the scrubbed pine table. A steaming pan sat on the old fashioned range, Harry recognised it the moment he had stepped into this room nearly three weeks ago, and he had seen exactly the same kitchen in the York Museum. Along with one from 1930 and another 1945, with another one that his mother had said was exactly like the one her parents had when she was a little girl in 1965. So as far as he was concerned this 'other world' was moving along the same path as his and Tina's own.

Only now he was more than ever convinced about Einstein's Theory of space and time as four related dimensions, and he also knew it would be highly unlikely that any explanation about the 'special theory' would be understood by anyone other than a scientist. He wondered if that was one of the certain people that Detective Woods was referring to, he could only hope so.

The conversation around the table consisted of 'how's' and 'what if's'. How would they find out about the strange way that Tina and Harry had arrived at this Raven-Scar? If the opportunity arose that the weird phenomena manifested itself, would Harry and Tina be able to be in a position to be there when it did? Cyril said that his beat was fairly extensive, that's why he had a bicycle so he would keep a very careful eye open and report immediately any strange dark fog, that could be the same that Harry and Tina had ridden into on the old rail track.

It was a bit tenuous they knew but what else could they do, but wait and hope that someday the strange fog would return to the same place or very near. How did these phenomena happen and what triggered it? It had to be linked somehow to whatever he, Harry, and the others, had on their person, all carried something that was digital and had small electrical pulses on a certain wave length, could that be it? Cyril suddenly had an idea; Harry had been saying that his physics teacher would not believe their story; he would think like people in this time, which Tina and Harry were having a joke, and Cyril's idea was simple.

'Harry lad, those things you call telephones, the one from Mr Broadbent showed some photographs, I mean I presume that's what they were. If yours and Tina's could take a few like, would that not be an advantage to you when you do find a way back?'

'Cyril that's brilliant, I'll take some more now.'

'No you won't my lad you'll wait until morning, this young lass is fair tuckered out and so are you by the look of you, come on now get washed and off to bed with you both. Look both of you, if it's any consolation Cyril and I do, in some way, believe that you are what you say you are. I don't understand what it is or how things happen as they do, but both 'on us do think that what you say is correct. And listen to me you can both stay here until, well until you know what to do, alright.'

'Agnes that's wonderful and we both thank you very much. I mean we could pay you but our money wouldn't buy anything would it?' Harry smiled at his words, Agnes and Cyril thought this highly amusing. It tickled Cyril no end to think that he a respected member of the community would be accused of passing forgeries, although the money was legitimate in another hundred years, he chortled all the way up to his bedroom. Tina and Harry could hear both Agnes and Cyril laughing mightily about counterfeit money.

It took another four days of riding around the town of Raven-Scar on their bikes, looking and searching for the elusive way back. That weird, cold, dry mist was not there when they needed it. It seemed like they would be lost in

Raven-Scar or the town that never was

this time, for more time than they wished, or forever, if nothing came about that could be used by them both.

They rode out onto the main road to Scarborough; the people in Raven-Scar became familiar with the two young people riding on strange looking bicycles around the town. Harry and Tina were somehow enjoying what was happening to them. Any other children they met they realised that as far as their education level was concerned they were miles ahead in Science, Maths, English, or any other matters of learning.

Both of them could speak French reasonably well. Tina could also speak German, something she insisted on learning, and physically, Tina and Harry came to the conclusion that they were a lot fitter than the children of the same age. Tina suggested that their diet was superior to what was available in the past, even though both of them made do with the occasional 'take-a-way' meal.

They both slept well that night; at least they had done something positive even though it was only by riding around Raven-Scar and its vicinity. Wanting to take a few more pictures on the dying mobile phones, but too apprehensive to do so, they needed at least some charge in their mobiles when they finally returned to their 2009, they hoped. They had forgotten Mr Broadbent's camera?

The following morning Harry and Tina were out at the same time as PC Whitaker, eager to find out if any of the three camera phones would have enough charge to take at least two pictures.

The problem was to make certain that any picture that they could take, even if only one was successful, had to be enough of an image to make their story believable. A ride down to the harbour gave them the perfect picture; standing on the tip of the pier they could see the 'tramway', the harbour and the length of the pier. Harry crossed his fingers and turned on his phone it 'bleeped' at him showing the battery state was not good enough for the camera; as he looked at the screen it gradually faded and went blank with a final 'bleep', it had run out of charge. Putting it in the pocket of his shortened long trousers he shrugged his shoulders.

'It's no use with my phone Tina? Try yours.'

Tina found that she did have sufficient charge and the camera flashed in the early morning gloom as she took her picture, clicking twice. 'Harry we have already taken some photos, don't you think we have enough? I'd like to leave some charge in the battery if poss. We may need it?'

'Don't take anymore then, let's have a look at the image? Hey that's great you can see everything very clearly'. Harry scrolled through the few images.

'Look at those of the town they are really good, and we have even got the Raven-Scar sign in there'.

The way back up to the town was not easy on a bike ,they had to push them back up the steep hill more or less to the top; resting they looked back to where they had come. The part of this town which Harry knew to be a golf course, showed all the streets leading down to the harbour, Britton Road, Norman Road, Dane Road, and Saxon Road.

' Tina if we could take a picture from here that would be the one to make people sit up and take notice, look at the houses all going down to where the harbour is, you can see the pier clearly from here, go on take a picture?'

'I can't Harry' Tina wailed. 'The battery is nearly expired. I want to keep some life in it. Oh Harry that would have been the best one. Hang on Harry did you bring the camera? The one that, that poor Mr Broadbent had on him'.

'Yes? It's here, let me see, the battery says low charge, it may be just enough, if I don't use the flash.'

Harry pressed the button the camera clicked and the image of Raven-Scar was in the bag, they both gazed at the image until the screen faded then bleeped. 'Well at least we have got something to show for our visit, I suppose we should call it a visit, what else can we call our being here? It's a pity we can't use the batteries in this camera in our phones, but they're too big'.

Raven-Scar or the town that never was

'I suppose a visit is as good as anything. Do you know Harry, I think if this place had been built in our world people would have visited it and holidayed here? I rather like it somehow, it's very peaceful just walking about and meeting different people. But what do they do I mean work, what work is there round here apart from farming, and fishing?'

'There are the Brickworks, the hotel, the railway all the B&Bs along Station Road and down to the harbour. There are the amusements on the pier: there's lots of work here Tina, if not here there must be a lot in Whitby. And what about the mines on the moors, there's a place called Loftus and then there's Guisborough'.

'But it would take people hours to get there; the roads are a bit like farm tracks'.

'The railway Tina, that runs all the way up the coast, right up to Redcar, even in our world it did that, you only have to look at the 'tile-map' at Scarborough Station to see that.'

'What tile map I haven't seen a map at the station, where is it?'

'Oh it's right on the end of Platform three. On the wall it shows all the rail lines in Yorkshire. Mr Yardley explained it to us when we went over to the rail Museum in York. It really is interesting to look at all the towns and villages. Well most villages had a station at some time linking them to the main lines that is until Mr Beeching gave them the chop. My dad says it was wilful destruction of a national asset, and I agree with him. I mean it would be wonderful if we could just take a train to wherever we wanted to go, instead of in the car. I don't like cars, I mean dad has one so has mum, but there are just too many on the roads, I mean where can we ride bikes really safely apart from the old rail line?'

'Harry the old rail line is anything but safe we got lost on it and ended up here remember, Safe indeed, Harry you have lost your marbles.' That remark made them both laugh at the absurd situation they found themselves in.

Arriving back at the Police Station they were surprised to find Detective Woods drinking tea and smoking his inevitable cigarette. Cyril was nowhere to be seen, he was out and about on his beat. Agnes came into the room and asked if either of them would like a cup of tea, both said 'yes please' they had been out for nearly three hours. The time was coming up to 9am no shops not even the café were open at this time. Detective Woods said he was very pleased to see the two 'time travellers' and he had some very interesting information. He lit another cigarette and, wreathed in smoke pulled out a small writing book from his pocket.

'I erm, took the liberty of having some items examined by experts in Leeds. The hospital there has a large science laboratory where a friend of mine works. This friend examined your money and to his surprise found that it was either a very, very good counterfeit, or was genuine but the ink and paper were, to his knowledge, unlike the materiels used now. The coins once again either excellent fakes or judging by the metal were genuine, but not negotiable. I had to resort to lying to him about where I had obtained the 'forgeries'.

Now this gun he was able to get some very good prints off of the weapon, nothing matches our files. But he was very interested in the gun itself, not having seen that type of barrel configuration and the name Gammo before, also the country of origin Spain. He found the marks interesting too there is a pressure mark on all guns be they huge guns on a warship or dainty little handbag guns. He found that the marks are not registered in any of the manuals he had. In other words Harry and Tina the gun should not exist?'

'Well it wouldn't would it. It hasn't been made yet. Not in this time anyway. What else did he find?' Harry was curious.

'Mmm, yes you mentioned a chap called Einstein. It appears that he does exist and, so the story goes, he's a mathematics genius and according to science journals he's working on something called, let me see I've written it down here ah, yes something related to time and space.'

'Yes E = $mc2$ the theory of relativity, time and space, four dimensions, I told you that, but Einstein will not bring out this theory until. Tina help me here, when did Einstein bring out the theory of relativity when was it published?' Tina shrugged her shoulders, Harry said. 'Got it 1915'.

Mr Woods puffed on his fourth cigarette looking at Harry closely he folded his little book.

'1915 is that what you said 1915? Young man this is 1909, how can you know what happens in 1915?'

'Exactly that's what we have been trying to tell you we do not belong here. When we rode into Raven-Scar that time we obviously went through some form of shift in time, don't ask me how I have no idea. But we obviously did or we would not be here would we. Our clothes are different, our bikes are like nothing you have here and our money, phones, cameras are from the future. We have to find that time-shift or we will not be able to return to our world and time, Einstein or no.'

'Harry and Tina, I can't in all honesty say I believe you, hand on heart I have to say that it is nonsense, but this is where I have to really decide on some peculiarities that have occurred. You for instance insist that you come from your future, not mine how is that possible? Even if time travel was possible how is it that your world is not like this one? Nearly so but not quite, also the presence of the dead man on the rail way, you young lady told me that he wasn't expecting any trains, which is not true is it? As we have seen there are trains on the railway. And the other thing, this bank robber coming and going like a wisp of smoke, you say he comes from your time? We don't know that do we?'

Lighting another cigarette he squinted at them through the smoke. Tina nearly said that in her world smoking was very much looked upon as being unsociable. The detective gave a cough, and adjusted his perch on the chair.

'And even though I say I can't believe you, I have to have I not? What other explanation is there?' He was interrupted by the appearance of Cyril, who looked very agitated.

'Ah, Sir, I've just come from the station the station master was on the phone he wanted to know where you were. You have to contact Whitby as soon as possible, it is very urgent.

CHAPTER 16

Detective Woods walked over to the police station counter. There was no desk in Cyril's office just this counter, a telephone, and his filing cabinets. Along with various items of police clothing, there was a water-proof black cape, a torch hung on a bracket on the wall, a spare pair of handcuffs and of course Cyril's bike propped against the wall. Picking up the phone, which needed two hands, he asked the operator for a number. Holding the speaker with his left hand he fumbled in one of his pockets, turning to Cyril saying.

'Constable get me paper and pencil please.' Writing rapidly with the occasional 'yes' and 'no' he finally replaced the ear piece onto its cradle, he re-read what he had written, his lips moving silently, looking at both Tina and Harry occasionally. Finally placing the piece of paper onto the counter top, he took out another cigarette from his packet and lit it up blowing smoke down his nose; taking another breath, this time he looked up to the ceiling and let the smoke drift out of his mouth; smoke lay in a wreath along the ceiling gradually dispersing. The Detective moved over to the large map on the wall behind the counter and looked at various places, turning to Cyril he asked.

'Constable where's Silpho?'

'It's about twelve miles from here on the edge of the moors, why?'

'A farmer, let me see his name, I've written it down, here, ah found it, name of Jack Withers. Farms at High Farm, do you know him?'

'I've heard of him but I don't know him.'

'Is he a truthful sort of chap would you say?'

'Oh aye, any of the farmers in that area are pretty good. Most of them come into Raven-Scar on market days to send livestock to market at either Whitby or Scarborough. Mind you a lot of the livestock round here goes over to Pickering, the market is bigger and the railway has direct links to Malton, what has he done?'

'Done! Oh nothing, but he called in at Scarborough Police Station and told a strange tale about a man camping out in the woods at the top of Silpho Bank. And listen to this, this Mr Withers says this chap rides some sort of funny motor-bicycle. Now, there can't be many 'funny motor-bicycles' round here can there. I'm just wondering about this. Harry can you explain to me what this so called 'funny' motor-bicycle could look like if, and I say if, it comes from your time. Not that I believe you entirely but just supposing?'

'Harry could draw it he's very good at drawing. Give him your pencil and some paper please. Did this farmer say what colour it was?'

'Yellow he says.'

Harry took the pencil from Tina and gave a rough sketch of a modern motorbike, he turned the paper over and he drew a much better picture.

'Have you a yellow crayon or something I can colour this with?' Cyril went into his kitchen and came back with coloured chalk.

'Will this do Agnes keeps some in a drawer in the kitchen?'

'Yes thank you.' Harry used the yellow chalk and the picture seemed to come to life so good was it. 'Look now it's finished this is more or less what I think it will look like, do you think so Tina?' She looked over his shoulder.

'Exactly, Harry that's a brilliant drawing you are clever.' Harry glowed with pride. Tina did not usually give out compliments, and he had to admit it wasn't a bad drawing at all. He handed it to Detective Woods who showed it to PC Whitaker, who's lips pursed in surprise and asked.

Raven-Scar or the town that never was

'How big would this machine be Harry?'

'In dimensions I suppose about as high as your bike Cyril but probably longer. Really I suppose not that much bigger than your bike actually. It would be a lot heavier of course because it has a motor, fuel tank and so forth. Oh and it can carry two people, just about.

Let me explain it to you, the front of the bike has two struts called suspension, they have springs in them and the rear suspension is hidden behind the rear wheel about here.'

He pointed his pencil at the drawing. 'And this is the motor I suppose you would call it an engine, but my dad says that engines run on rails, anyway those are the handlebars with all the controls on them.'

'Where is the gear lever lad? It's usually on the side of the tank along with the oil pressure tank and pump.' Cyril was knowledgeable.

'That's down here near the footrest; the oil is in the motor and there is not a hand pump. On the other side is the rear brake. If the bike looks like this one in the drawing then it's called a trail bike or enduro bike; which means that it can go virtually anywhere, even over the moors. Anybody riding this machine can go anywhere, even if there are no roads and, if this chap is where this Mr Withers says he is, then he must have found a way to come and go through time. How he does it we would love to know, we have to know, and then we could go back. Find him Mr Woods sir and let us ask him?'

Cyril still wanted to know more about this wonderful machine from the future, maybe not his future but somebody's future at least.

'Harry how fast can this machine go and how far can it travel?' he asked. Harry thought about the question before he answered.

'I'm not too sure really Cyril but I would think the bike would easily do say, ninety miles an hour maybe a hundred, and the range mmm! Say a hundred miles give or take. As I said Cyril I'm not all that sure but I would think those figures are about correct. Don't forget also that this bike can travel over very rough ground and it would do about fourty to fifty miles an hour even over the roughest ground.'

'Nearly a hundred miles an hour, Harry that's faster than most trains I'll have you know and travelling nearly a hundred miles, that's unbelievable. Fifty miles an hour over the moors, by 'eck he must be a brave man to do that, either that or very stupid. That's amazing what you have just told us Harry.' Cyril was very impressed about the future, yes well quite!

CHAPTER 17

The detective knew, he just knew that the man camping at Silpho Bank had to be the wanted man. The man who's fingerprints were on the sawn off shot-gun, It had to be. The description of the weird bike he rode was exactly as seen by witnesses, and if this person is able to move through time. Ridiculous he knew. But if he did then Tina and Harry's story was correct. Mr Woods was not a physicist; he was just an ordinary copper who had the ability to unravel a problem. He knew that now he was beginning to unravel this problem.

He deliberately got in touch with the criminal department in Leeds; there he had spoken to a detective who was very knowledgeable about science and especially physics.

"Yes" he was told. Men like Einstein and Planck were working on mathematics that had never before been subject to intense scientific scrutiny "No I'm sorry Detective, I can't say in all certainty that travel through time was or is possible. At the present time, excuse the pun please, only in the imagination of men like Verne and Wells. But, and this is a big but, if what I read in scientific papers is correct, it may theoretically be possible, but only in theory."

That was enough for detective Woods he had a hunch like all good policemen that this felt right. Picking up the telephone again he asked the operator for a connection with the Army Barracks in Scarborough, he waited until the operator had made his connection. All calls had to go through a switch board operated by, usually, a woman who would plug in a number of cables to make a connection.

'Hello this is Detective Woods from Leeds Police Department who am I speaking to? Ah! Good afternoon

Colonel I have a favour to ask of you and your men. We have a situation that a while ago a bank manager was shot and killed in a robbery. The perpetrator escaped on a motor-cycle,,, Yes that's right,,, No we did not have a vehicle at the time only the horse drawn police van,,, Yes I know that but we don't have much call for a motor vehicle, we do have a van of course but as for trying to chase a motor-cycle it just is not possible. What I am thinking is that this chap is camping on top of Silpho Bank,,, Yes that's right,,, A farmer called Withers High Top Farm contacted us when he came into Scarborough,,,,Certainly,,, I've only got four men and one of those has to police Raven-Scar.

Yes sir what do I need? a small group of men who could stalk this chap and capture him is that possible?,,, Yes I understand that permission has to come from above I have the same problem,,,, Thank you,,, Yes the operator will put you through to this telephone in Raven-Scar. I'm much obliged colonel. Oh and one more thing this criminal has a motor-cycle and could be armed,,,, Why I say that is because he dropped a shot-gun at the bank and we have his dabs on it,,,,Pardon ,,,,Yes shot-gun shortened,,, Cutting the barrels off of course,,,Thank you I'll be here.'

He replaced the telephone with the ear pieced back onto its cradle.

'That was Colonel Mathers at Scarborough barracks, he is going to telephone me back in one hour, Constable can you give me details of this area around Silpho please?'

Cyril arranged the map so that all of them could see in more detail that part of the forest on the edge of the moors. It was fairly remote, with access through a village called Burniston which sat on the road from Scarborough to Whitby. The roads were really farm tracks up to the edge of the forest especially to where the small hamlet of Silpho stood.

'Looks a bit tricky to get there constable, seems we need horses to reach it. At least there seems to be plenty of cover for a surprise attack from the army.' At that moment

Raven-Scar or the town that never was

the telephone rang, Detective Woods lifted the ear piece up and gave his name; listening for some five minutes with the occasional 'mmm' and aha' he said a final 'thank you Colonel.'

Jiggling the ear piece cradle he finally got through to the operator, asking to be connected to the Police Station in Whitby.

'Hello is that Sergeant Fellows? Ah excellent. Detective Woods here,,, Yes I'm still in Raven-Scar. Listen Sergeant, can you get hold of a couple of horses, good enough to get us to Silhpo,,,Yes that's right. I'm pretty sure this is the chap that shot the bank manager and now he's holed up there somewhere near the forest,,, Camping out so we are told,,, Pardon? Armed well I would think so, obviously he has used a shot-gun previously so there is nothing to indicate that he won't have one now. We shall go on that premise certainly,,, Ah!, good man,,, Let me see the next train is due in?' turning to Cyril he raised his eyebrows.

'Half an hour sir,' replied Cyril.

'Half an hour Sergeant let me say I can be there in just over an hour, good man; oh one more thing, break out a couple of revolvers will you, Webley's will do fine .32's will suffice, thank you Sergeant.'

Agnes came into the Police Station office with tea and biscuits, and as they sat round the small table, Detective woods explained his strategy.

'Colonel Mathers says he has six trained men who are just right for this situation. One of them is an experienced sniper, seemingly he fought in the Boer campaign. The others are all skilled in stalking, so I have asked Sergeant Fellows to provide two horses one for myself and the other for one of his men. Constable I want you to remain here in Raven-Scar. It's a possibility that this chap may be making his way here. May be he might make an attempt at either the bank or the jewellers, what's the name?'

'Marlow's' replied Agnes who was still in the room.

'Thank you Mrs Whitaker, oh yes and thank you for the tea and biscuits it's very kind of you.'

'Think nothing of it Detective, and please call me Agnes I'm not used to Mrs Whitaker. Besides it's not often we get a Detective from Leeds. In fact I don't think we have ever had one from Leeds, it's such a long way to come.'

'That is not much of a problem Agnes; I can be here within four hours the train connections are very good you know. Now we can soon get to the 'seaside' from Leeds, either to Scarborough or Whitby. Change at Malton through Pickering and hey presto, here we are. Anyway back to our problem, you two youngsters will remain here with PC Whitaker. No arguments please, this is for your own safety. Do you know I'm going to enjoy this arrest? Just imagine arresting a person from the future, what am I saying the impossible may be possible. Ridiculous.'

'But what if it is a possibility that we are correct Detective then you will have to believe us, will you not?'

Harry was losing his patience with Detective Woods. The obvious was staring him in the face and he still did not acknowledge the fact. Yes he did realise that this situation sounded very far-fetched, but not as farfetched as it was to him and Tina. And besides whatever the Detective had said he, Harry, was somehow going to Silpho come what may.

He had to be there, it would be a tragedy for him and Tina if the soldiers, or the police for that matter, shot the 'bank robber'. They had no firm evidence to prove that it was him camped near Silpho, just the words of a farmer. If he was killed then the two 'time travellers' would be in real trouble, with no way of finding out what the bank robber had knowledge of.

If the man resisted he could be shot dead by one of the soldiers; now that would be the worst of scenarios, their one and only chance would be lost, and he and Tina would be trapped in this world and time. On reflection he supposed that it would not be too bad, they would have no parents, or friends unless they made new ones, no that was the unthinkable, they would have no proof of birth, education or where they said they lived, the problems seemed insurmountable, Harry would have to tell Tina all that he was thinking.

Detective Woods was talking quietly to Cyril; he would be leaving Raven-Scar and catching the train through to Whitby shortly so he had to have everything in place. If the 'bank robber' and he was certain that this person was he, made for Raven-Scar then he wanted the PC to be sure that he knew exactly what had to be done. Cyril would be issued with a revolver just in case. Harry beckoned to Tina to follow him out-side, standing on the pavement with the wind drifting a slight mist around the houses he explained to Tina what he had in mind.

That he had to find the man camped out in the forest preferably before the soldiers or the police found him.

'Just one simple thing Harry, how are you getting there, by bike?'

'Exactly yes, I can ride up there I've thought it through and I can get back to Scalby up the bank and down into Hackness, then up Silpho Bank. I've climbed that road before, it's very steep but I think I can make it before the police get there by horse-back.'

'Just a minute what do you mean by I, there is no I, in this Harry, I'm going too. Do you think I'd stay here while you go chasing an armed man then think again Harry, no way are you going without me.'

'But it's...'

'No buts Harry I'm going, so let's talk about how we get there quickly. I mean the ride to Scalby from here would take us what about an hour? Especially on these roads none of them are brilliant are they? One of the reasons why we travel on the old track is because it's more or less level not hilly like the roads. Also the climb from Hackness is like scaling mount Everest it's that steep, it would take us at least two or more hours to get there, a horse would get there quicker across country.'

'I suppose it would but the Detective has to get back to Whitby, find the horse and then ride over the moors through the forest to get to the top of Silpho Bank. All right if you insist on coming, don't blame me if you don't make it, one of us has to contact this man to find out if he knows how to come and go through time. Tina he has to know or else we are stuck here, do you want that?'

'Obviously not; don't be so negative Harry, I'll make it don't worry all we have to do is get our bikes and get going as soon as we can oh,' she groaned. 'I've just remembered our bikes are locked up in one of the cells, how shall we get round asking Cyril to let us have them? They're locked up to stop us trying to ride down the railway track, damn I'd forgotten that.'

Tina never used strong language, damn was about all she would say. Harry swore under his breath he had forgotten that as well. Where did Cyril keep the cell keys? The clothes they had on especially those that Tina wore where not suitable for riding over moorland especially as the mist was becoming denser.

Time was pressing on, they had to get their own clothes and find something warmer. Harry could keep the jacket that Agnes had bought from the 'jumble sale' but, for Tina, that was a different matter, the long coat she had would hamper her cycling. She looked around the room they were the only ones there now, both of the Policemen had gone to the rail station. Agnes was back in her kitchen, Harry said to look for the cell keys which they proceeded to do, their search through draws and cupboards proved fruitless.

'Harry have you any idea what I can cover myself with?' Harry noticed the black police cape hanging on it's peg the old style cape covered the shoulders and down to the waist of a tall man, would it do for Tina? He lifted the cape from its hook, underneath hanging there where the cell keys.

Raven-Scar or the town that never was

Breathing a sigh of relief he opened the door to the cell in which he had been sleeping and took out all their clothes.

'Come on put these on, use Cyril's cape to cover yourself, it should keep you warm and dry, come on get moving.'

'Not while you are in the room Harry I can't change while you're here.'

'Sorry I'll go into my cell' Harry grinned at Tina who gave him a baleful look. Both quickly dressed in their own clothes Harry put on his jacket, it fitted him reasonably well, whilst Tina draped the black cloak around her. It fastened at the neck with a small chain, and had three buttons down the front, fastening the cloak up it came down below her waist but it was lined with warm materiel.

'How do I look?' she asked Harry.

'Like a small policeman, no sorry you look ok, honestly at least it will keep the mist off of you and it looks reasonably warm, how do you feel in it?'

'Fine, and no more remarks about a small copper. Harry have you seen the time? We have no chance of getting to Silpho before dark and believe me it is very dark up there and we have no lights, well not good enough to ride on the roads around there, so what do we do now?'

'We go now.'

'I have just told you that we won't get there before it's too dark to see, did you hear me?'

'Yes I did, I know it will be dark but what else can we do wait for morning? By then the soldiers will have found the man and hopefully not shot him but arrested him, then we have no chance of asking him how and where he can come and go so easily. Tina we have to go now even if we have to sleep out on the moors. We can fill our water bottles, and take those biscuits that are left, look in that drawer under the counter there's a bar of chocolate there we can take that.'

'Fry's chocolate is that all we can take, I can eat that in two minutes.'

'Pig, so can I come on grab it and let's go.'

Tina was not in the least convinced that they could be alright out on the moors in the dark.

'Harry did the detective say there was a revolver here?'

'I don't think so, he told the constable in Whitby to get two, one for him and one for Cyril just in case; besides I have no idea how to use one, come on we have to get going.'

Pushing their bikes out of the police station they were soon riding down Station Road into Scarborough Road over the rail tunnel and on towards the village of Cloughton.

Stopping for a drink Tina asked if it would be easier and quicker if they went through Harwood Dale. Harry agreed, especially as by now dusk was falling. There was no chance of them reaching their destination before it became too dark to see. Harry's enthusiasm and his need to speak to the so called bank robber had meant he hadn't thought things through clearly.

Tina was correct, and he knew now they either turned back, or carried on and spent the night out in the open. There was a possibility that they could find shelter in a barn as the farms were dotted with outbuildings. They could not go back so they had little choice but to carry on and hope.

Darkness was total, once they neared the forest. Tina was glad of the police cloak, it was water and wind proof, Harry was not as lucky as the wool jacket he was wearing was soon saturated with the slight mist. They had turned off their cycle-lamps to conserve the batteries, but without their glow they could not see very much. The track they were on was, in their time, the road through to Silpho Top but now a century earlier and in another time; it was nothing but a farm track which was very muddy and slippery.

Harry looked at his watch it was 11-30 pm; they had to find shelter. The mist was closing in and becoming thick and menacing, and very cold. Harry was starting to shiver in his sodden jacket, and suddenly they stumbled into bushes.

Raven-Scar or the town that never was

'Harry I think we should walk; if we can find a wall we could shelter behind it, ouch! Harry I think I've found a wall or a building of some sort, yes it's a building.'

A voice came out of the dark, speaking quietly with just an ounce of menace in it.

'Shhh! Hold very still, do not move or make a sound, I have a gun!' the voice chilled Tina. She turned slowly to see if she could find where the voice came from. It was too dark and the mist was now turning to rain, she could hear Harry's teeth chattering with the cold.

'T-tina I've g,g,got to f,f,find s,s,somewhere t,to get w,w,warm.'

Harry was heading towards hypothermia, if they couldn't get out of the rain. The voice hissed in Tina's ear she gasped, she had no idea that whoever it was, was so close to her.

'Be very, very quiet hold my hand and follow me.'

Tina fumbled for Harry's hand, finding it in the dark it was shaking so much that she nearly let go of it. The other hand she was holding was very firm on hers and was pulling her forward. She had little idea of the ground under her feet and stumbled over grassy tussocks: the hand let go of hers and a light came out of the dark, she could see the shadowy figure of a tall man. He had opened a broken down door into a field barn, suitable for sheep.

But now in the light of a fire which crackled and spat in the middle of the one room she could see a bright yellow motor-cycle propped up against one wall. They had found the one man they wanted desperately to see, the tall figure, laid down a sawn off shotgun.

'Now I don't know who you two are, or how you came here on a night like this? So, which farm are you from and why abroad on this lousy night? I want answers and I want them now.'

Tina knew that Harry was in no condition to say anything legibly as he was shaking with the cold; she helped him off with his sodden jacket and looked around for somewhere to hang it, the man pointed to a protruding brick in the wall.

'Hang it on there, pull that lump of wood closer to the fire then he, what's his name?'

'Harry'

'Right then Harry can get closer to the fire, what's your name any way?'

'Tina' Harry sat down as near to the fire as he could. The fire was not all that big, but with the field-barn being fairly small the fire generated enough heat to feel reasonably warm, Tina carried on talking. 'We know who you are and where you come from.'

'What do you mean know who I am? I've never seen you before and I very much doubt that you do know where I'm from, you would be amazed if you knew, you really would in fact you just would not believe me, I find it hard to believe it myself.'

'2009, that's where you come from and I can't believe it either.' Tina's steady gaze made the man feel uncomfortable. He sat down onto the floor of the barn, looking at Tina then Harry.

'How the hell did you know that? And how did you get here? I suppose you came on your bike's eh.' he laughed at his joke,

'Yes we did, they're out there we dropped them on the floor outside of a wall, then we sort of stumbled onto this building, or more to the point we stumbled onto you the one man we had to find.'

'Had to find, listen young lady nobody knows I'm here?'

'Yes they do the Police for one and the Army for another; there is a search party out for you. No don't interrupt me please, the Police know who you are, you robbed a bank and shot the bank manager didn't you?'

'I shot at him he wouldn't open the safe.'

'You shot at him and killed him.'

The strangers face paled.

Raven-Scar or the town that never was

'Killed him I didn't intend to do that I thought I'd shot into the wall behind him. The bloody fool moved but I didn't think I'd done that. My god if they catch me I'll be jailed for a long time.'

'No you won't you will be hanged. This is still in the time of capital punishment, and hanging is what will happen to you. The reason why we wanted to find you before either the Police or Army, by the way they have instructions to shoot you if you offer any resistance, is to find out how you can come and go into this time and this world. Harry and I realise when speaking to people here, that not only have we come back in time, but into another dimension, the same world and time but sort of skewed in another direction. Oh don't ask us we don't know either. All we do know is if we can't find that time portal then we have no chance of returning to our time and yours if you're lucky.'

Tina had said what she had to say, and then asked. 'What's your name? You know ours so what's yours? I want to know the man we are sheltering with if he is a killer.' The man winced at this.

'Jeffrey Lawson, that's my name, call me Jeff, I can't believe that somebody else found out how to come here, what happened to you?'

By this time Harry had stopped shivering and now took up their story explaining how the two of them rode on the old rail track coming off at Ravenscar in their time going into the café and finding themselves in another time and world, and all the rest that had happened to them including their fruitless search for the way back into 2009. Harry had to ask the one question that had to be asked.

'How did you get here and more to the point how did you return to 2009?'

'I didn't, I've been camping out since I got here, not exactly here but in the forest or in a barn like this.'

'You mean you don't know how to get back?'

'Sorry no haven't a clue, like you I rode up the rail track then I entered the tunnel.'

'Tunnel you mean the one at Ravenscar?'

'Certainly yes, just as I went into it I had this weird feeling there was a very dense mist or fog, but not like normal mist, it was very cold, colder than a mist should be, and the strangest thing was unlike normal mist this one was not wet, it was cold and extremely dry. I thought at the time it was weird, but not as weird as the blinking train that came out of the tunnel towards me, that shook me up I can tell you I thought I'd had it I only just missed the thing, or it just missed me, then it stopped at the station. I couldn't understand it, I mean trains haven't run there for 40 odd years. I walked into the tunnel and the mist was dispersing, it was swirling as it moved down the tunnel, I walked out as the train was moving off, people were talking and I could hear horses, then an old car pulled up outside of the station. I thought hang on this is a film set.'

'Same as us that's what we thought, when we went into the café.'

'Ah, no I never went in there I could see a copper on the station platform, I thought he looked odd, that's what made me think I was in a film set. Then I thought how the heck did they get a train up here there aren't any lines. That was the next shock I could see the lines running away down the track towards Scarborough, then I walked through the station. I'd propped my Suzuki up against the side of the tunnel wall. There were loads of people moving around then the train moved off; by this time I really thought I was going bonkers.

Going out of the station I just stood, unable to believe what I was looking at, the streets, the houses, people walking around, horse and carts with a couple of hansom cabs standing near the kerb, all the streets were cobbled. I knew that was not right, some people looked at me as if I had come from another world well as you know I had, same as you if what you say is right. I was dressed like this you see with all my clobber on straight from the bike and with a crash helmet in my hand and I could see the copper moving towards me so I scarpered back into the tunnel and rode through to the other end following the lines got to the end and the lines stretched out before me.

I knew then that I was living in a nightmare; I tried to find that weird mist but no such luck. Then I hid the bike and walked back into the town: as I did I noticed the town sign "Raven-Scar the new holiday destination. With links to Scarborough and Whitby" I tell you I nearly fainted at this, but I had to get my head around this. I thought if I'm not in a film set what other explanation was there? I'm fairly knowledgeable about science, so I went back through my mind, trying to remember anything out of the ordinary. The only thing, well until the train that is, was that peculiar mist that was the only obvious thing, so I thought straight away that I had come across a phenomenon of time and space. I sort of knew what happened but the how was and still is beyond me. All I know is that as far as I'm aware I, and now you, are stuck in this time zone: as far as I'm concerned I can live with it. Apart from the fact that my bike will run out of petrol soon, I can use whatever I have to say buy a house somewhere, and live quietly.'

'Just a minute you said the train came at you when you rode towards the tunnel, why didn't the train go through the time zone, whatever it's called?' Harry asked.

'I don't know? I think it has something to do with our mobiles, it's just a thought I've had recently and it made me think, electricity may be the answer although it has to be on a certain wave length.'

'But the trains have electricity on them don't they?' asked Tina.

'No I remember now in the café Tina the two train drivers asked for matches to light the oil lamps don't you remember?'

'Oh yes now you mention it I do. But the trains have lights on the front don't they?' Tina questioned this statement.

'As I have just said to you I think it is our mobile phones that trigger this 'thing' off?' Mr Lawson reminded them.

'But if you robbed the bank and the jewellers you didn't take any money, why?'

'That's obvious isn't it? I thought I could find a way to return to my time, so what good would money be to me. No it had to be gold, gold coins and jewellery, now I suppose I'll have to take money instead.'

'You mean you're going to rob again?'

'Of course what else, I don't exist in this time and world do I? No more than you do so what difference does it make. Anyway come on its nearly two in the morning and after all that talking I'm tired, oh, before you think of escaping, don't bother, you won't get far this place is very remote.'

You forgot about the gun?' Tina said.

'Gun what are you on about, what gun?'

'The one you left at the bank after you shot the manager.'

'So, what about it?'

'It's a modern gun, not made in 1909, we were taken into custody, although as it turned out it wasn't really, by P C Whitaker in Raven-Scar. We've been there ever since 'it' happened. Then we went with him to Whitby where we met a detective from Leeds. Because of the killing and the strange way you disappeared the police had to call in a specialist and Detective Woods is just that. He sent the gun for examination, found it had strange markings on it something to do with pressure, is that right Harry?'

'Yes, not only that but your finger prints are on it, all they have to do is match those with yours and bingo, you will be charged with murder and robbery, so unless you want to be hanged you had better help us find that strange mist again, then we can all get back. Hopefully, they know that the gun does not belong in this time, we told them all about it and us and they believe us, well some of them do. We showed them our mobile phones and a hiker was killed by a train it just happened that he came across the same

Raven-Scar or the town that never was

mist that we three found. His trouble was that he was coming walking from Whitby when he sort of occupied the same place as the train poor man, still he wouldn't have known very much when the train hit him. But he had binoculars and a mobile phone; better still he had a camera in his rucksack, so we were able to show the few people that were beginning to believe us, the future, then they did. By the way where did you get that gun?'

'I had it with me I do, did; some shooting on the moors' Jeff grinned maliciously. 'Illegally of course, then I thought "what an opportunity" I robbed the jeweller then realised I could do the same with a few banks. So I broke into a workshop and cut the barrels and butt off of it, very handy it was too, I was a fool to leave it behind but I had to get out of that bank sharpish, get on the bike and scram.

Now for your info, I have another one, this time one that belongs to this world. The farmer who found out it's gone will have some explaining to the Police to do. Look let's talk more in the morning, I'm going to get some kip, you should do the same, and sorry I've no blankets you'll have to share that cape g 'night. Ahh one more thing, if you think of running away, and you also think I won't use this gun, remember I can only hang for one murder so two more makes no difference to me. Sleep tight.'

Harry and Tina draped the police cape over themselves and snuggled closer so as to keep warm. They drifted into a troubled sleep, wondering what the next few hours would bring.

CHAPTER 18

Harry was shaken awake by a man in battle-dress uniform. With bleary eyes he tried to remember where he was, sitting up he made out the shape of Tina still asleep under the black cape; he shivered from the cold, the fire was out, so was Jeff Lawson, he sat upright.

'He's gone, he's gone to find a way back?'

'Easy lad, takes it steady, here have a drink of tea, it's nice and hot. I'm Sergeant Train of the Yorkshire Light Infantry, and we've been watching out for your chap. He gave us the slip during the night but we'll get the blighter. We camped in one of the fields over there,' he said pointing out of the door. 'We had a Detective Woods with us, he rode up from Whitby do you know him? And what's the name of this bloke that the police are looking for?'

'Yes we know the detective; we left him in Raven-Scar and came here on our bikes, and the man is called Jeff Lawson.'

'Why lad is there someone else here?'

Harry uncovered the shape of Tina who, startled by voices, came awake quicker than Harry had done. She looked at the soldier, not quite believing her eyes. Harry held out the mug of still hot tea, she accepted it without thinking, the hot liquid warmed her instantly, and she scrambled into a kneeling position looking round for Mr Lawson.

'He's gone Tina; crikey look he's left his motor bike. I wonder why? He won't get far without it.'

'He probably didn't want to make any noise, he must have known we were looking for him and probably he had seen us on the moors. We had torches with us so we could spot him. It were a bit misty though but we had an idea he was around here; the information we had from the farmer

Raven-Scar or the town that never was

made us think this was the likely spot for him to hide out. Now come with me and have something to eat.'

'We can't we have to find him.'

'No you don't young lady you have to eat first; it's not much just bacon and eggs, and we don't go hungry in this Army you know.'

The Sergeant's grin made Harry and Tina feel more comfortable, he gave them both a blanket to put round their shoulders as he escorted them out of the barn along the farm track and into a field where three small tents had been erected. Outside of one, to their delight, was a fire with one of the soldiers holding a pan and frying breakfast.

Harry looked at his watch, it was 6am; the morning was still misty but the sun was trying to shine through the mist. It looked like it could be a much better day than yesterday. They both sat down onto small folding chairs, each was offered a tin plate and another mug of the sweet tea; the cook ladled eggs and bacon onto the plates and added a couple of slices of bread. Their hunger made them start eating immediately, the Fry's chocolate bar had long ago been eaten and now they realised how famished they were.

While they ate, the Sergeant conversed with the other soldiers; there were eight in total, four of them were already fully dressed and had packs on their backs, ammunition pouches slung across their shoulders, they nodded in unison to what the Sergeant was saying to them, then turning around they walked off out of the field and disappeared into the forest.

Sergeant Train sat down with a mug of tea in his hands, speaking to the cook who happened to be a corporal. He gave instruction for the camp to be cleared. Turning his attention to Harry and Tina, he inspected their dishevelled appearance, and showed no surprise at the way they were dressed, to the soldier shorts and a shirt was standard running gear.

'It's a bit rough out here when it gets dark, how did you two come here? And what do you know about this chap we are looking for? Apart from the fact that he has killed a bank manager, we know little else so you can probably fill me in with a few more details. Ah, yes the detective say's that you two are stupid for doing what you did, so what did you do? And what is that peculiar machine back there in the barn. I know what it is supposed to be, a motor bicycle, but not like 'owt I've seen before and we found another two-wheeled thing resting against the wall behind the field barn, is it yours?'

Tina spoke first, Harry was still mopping up his breakfast, she explained as simply as she could how and why they had ridden up to Silpho not explaining nor even trying to explain time travel, that would come later; all she told the Sergeant was enough to put him in the picture. She said, yes the two-wheeled thing in the barn was a motor-bicycle; the Sergeant shook his head, doing the same with her explanation on the other two-wheeled machine, this time her mountain bike.

Harry's bike had gone. Mr Lawson had seen to that and was more than likely now riding it on his way to somewhere.

Harry's brain went 'ping' Lawson was going somewhere definite, why? Suppose he had lied to them about him remaining here in this time; was it possible that he knew how to come and go through time? Where was he heading now? It had to be something to do with either the tunnel at Raven-Scar or somewhere towards Whitby, but still on the line.

After Lawson robbed the bank and shot the manager, witnesses said that he disappeared. He would have ridden down the rail line until he came back to the tunnel. About ten miles Harry thought: yes that was it he knew where the time gap was, he had lied to them he did come and go, he had no intention of staying in this time and why should he? It was too easy for him to just travel through to this time,

Raven-Scar or the town that never was

and as for Saying he would buy a house and stay here, that was poppycock.

No, Lawson was onto something that he thought only he knew about, his leaving now was to find the way back and all would be well, he would not have to face a trial or the threat of being hanged. And his ill-gotten gains would be used in 2009. Gold was at an all-time high and if he had gathered enough of it and also the coins he has stolen, then he would be a darn sight better off financially than he was before his lucky chance of suddenly finding himself in another time and world.

He was a man of opportunity that was certain, and he could become rich, thief or no. Harry had to admire him, he must have had one great shock at his predicament then finding that he could come and go through time, he made the most of it. He had committed murder for his own gain and he should face the consequences of that and be jailed. That of course depended on which of the two times he would be in. If here in 1909 then he most definitely would hang. But he could not be brought to justice in 2009, how could he? *No one would believe neither Harry nor Tina that Lawson shot and killed a man in 1909: that was preposterous.* Harry was determined that Lawson would remain in this time and face up to his misdeeds.

'Tina I know where Lawson is going,' he explained all that he had been thinking. That Lawson knew a way to pass through time, that he had lied to them and that now he was more than likely on his way to Raven-Scar.

'I think you are right Harry, I thought he didn't show much surprise at his saying he could not find a way back. If that had been me I would have gone bonkers. He must know how to do it, we've got to find him and make him tell us how.' The Sergeant had been listening to this conversation with an amused expression on his face, now he asked the question.

'What on earth do you mean going back? And what has time got to do with it?' As a soldier he was used to many things but what he was hearing alarmed him. These two strange young people, spoke as if they came from the future; impossible of course. but then he glanced at the bright yellow machine propped against the wall of the barn, one of the soldiers had brought it out to look at, he had a feeling that something was not quite as it seemed. This machine most certainly did not belong here, it was nothing like any machine he knew of and the Army did use motor- bicycles for certain duties but they were as far removed from this machine as flying pigs!

'Just a minute you two, let me ask you what you're talking about? You mentioned finding the way back and time, are you telling me you come from somewhere else not in 1909, but the future?'

In unison Tina and Harry answered the Sergeant.

'Yes, we don't belong here, not in this time and hard though it is to believe, we found, quite by chance, that we went back in time. Not only that, but ended up in another world, very much like ours but different in a lot of ways.'

They took it in turns to explain to the amazed Sergeant and by this time the other four soldiers, who sat quietly smoking listening to the words of science so far beyond their thinking, that they accepted it. Their worldly experience made them aware that peculiar things happened for no particular reason so time travel was just another of those peculiarities, nothing unusual in that.

It was only twenty years ago that a German called Benz had made a moving vehicle using what he said was an internal combustion engine, now they could see automobiles on the road. Very expensive toys of course, nothing would be better than the good old horse.

But on reflection did not steam trains now criss- cross the country to all points of the compass, now that was the future. Steam-trains gave people the means to travel where ever they chose. Also there was a rumour that in America, two brothers were experimenting trying to use a heavier than air machine to lift off the ground; far-fetched of course

Raven-Scar or the town that never was

it would never happen how could it? Metal and wood was far heavier than air and it was impractical to think that men could fly. Balloons, yes, hot air ones, for sure, but an engine and wings, no never, still times were changing.

CHAPTER 19

Tina and Harry stopped speaking as the soldiers suddenly jumped up grabbing their rifles. In the distance they could hear the sharp crack of rifles being fired, with the answering bang of a shotgun, the Sergeant shouted at one of his men.

'Private Henson, find out what's going on?' The young soldier started off at a run jumping over the wall and disappearing into the forest. 'Henson is our runner he'll find out what's happened.'

'Why don't you use your radio?' asked Tina, the look of amusement on the face of the Sergeant told her all she wanted to know, there were no radios in 1909, certainly not used by the Army. Marconi was awarded the Noble Prize for physics in 1909, but as for portable radios no chance. Half an hour later the sound of a motor-cycle chugging up the hill towards them, on the back holding on very tightly to the military despatch rider was Henson,. He jumped off the rear of the motor-cycle, saluted and made his report.

'Corporal Hall showed me a man that had shot at them. They returned fire and wounded him in the leg: the man was riding a peculiar machine, he said it was his bicycle, Corporal Hall showed it to me. I have to say Sergeant it's nothing like I remember bicycles.'

'No it's mine, he took it while we were all of us sleeping'. Harry showed concern but he had another plan, he would tell Tina when they were on their own.

'Oh, right, anyway the bloke is with them right now; they want to know what has to be done with him. I hitched a ride with the DR, he's come up from Scarborough to report back to the Colonel. What are we going to do now Sarge?'

'Corporal are we all packed and ready?' the corporal answered that they were ready to go. 'Right Henson I want

Raven-Scar or the town that never was

you to stay with Tina and Harry they can get a lift back in the lorry; what's the road like up to here, can it make it over these roads?'

'Not to the field Sarge it's pretty muddy but that's no problem we can carry what we have, the driver will help us; what are we to do with this thing?' pointing at the Suzuki.

'Tina and I can ride it back behind the truck,' Harry wanted time to explain to Tina his idea.

'Right lads that's all settled, Henson stays and helps load the lorry. Are you sure you can ride this thing Harry?' Harry said that he rode his fathers' bike around the fields, which satisfied the Sergeant.

'Harry!' Tina whispered.

'Shh, tell you in a minute.' Harry was waiting until the army lorry came and then 'plan A' would be put into action. Corporal Henson offered a cigarette to Tina and Harry, both shook their heads; shrugging Henson lit his own and sat down on one of the army packs; looking at the two young people he blew a stream of smoke, out of his nostrils. He admired Tina it was very, very unusual for a girl as young as her to parade in shorts, still young people changed all the time so he supposed this was a new way of attire, especially if riding one of those weird cycles.

'How come you're mixed up in all this, did this chap Lawson really kill a bank manager?'

'He certainly did, he robbed the bank of gold and bullion'

'Not money? Why not money? I mean if I robbed a bank I would take all the cash I could, and make sure no one would catch me.' Henson puffed on his cigarette, thinking of all he could do with money taken from a bank. He had never been inside of a bank, why would he, his money just about allowed him to buy a few drinks on Saturday nights and not much left over after that. 'That yellow thing over there is it really a motor-cycle? And where did this Lawson get something like that? It looks very, well special, and the name it sounds different, where is Suzuki?'

'Not where more like what? It's Japanese, there are four main motor-cycle makers in Japan, and this is one of them, do you want to know the others?' Henson said not really as he didn't believe them he said they were pulling his leg, Japan. Come on that was the other side of the world and he had never heard of anything being sold in England that came from Japan.

Harry told him to wait and see if things went according to the way of the world, well his world, Japan would make a huge difference to what would be manufactured in the future, or not. Harry remembered that this world may not turn out the same as the one he and Tina had left. And trying to talk to Henson about space and time, let alone Einstein's theory, would be a complete waste of time, so he walked over to the Suzuki; fortunately Lawson had left the key in the ignition.

"Made in Japan" most things made in Harry and Tina's world came either from Japan or China. This world, although similar to their own, was different in so many ways. There may not be any wars in this world's future. A thought struck Harry, what if he could come back in say eighty years time, just to find out if there was a massive difference, it was an idea he told himself.

Turning the key and pressing the 'start' button the motor fired up and settled down to a steady beat. Harry twisted the throttle and the crackling sound from the exhaust made Henson draw back, Harry jumped onto the saddle and found he could just about reach the ground on tip-toe. He put the bike into gear and opened the throttle it leapt forward and Harry shot away across the muddy field with the back wheel spinning, turning round he returned with a big grin on his face.

'Want to come for a ride Henson?

The soldier climbed onto the pillion seat and the bike roared out of the field onto the farm track. Turning round Harry twisted the throttle as far as it would go; the Suzuki was in second gear and immediately the front wheel left the

Raven-Scar or the town that never was

ground, it came down with a thud and they shot off back to where Tina stood at the field entrance, stopping suddenly. Harry waited until Henson staggered off the back of the bike.

'That is an unbelievable machine, how fast did we go Harry?'

'Forty miles an hour,' Harry told him, knowing full well that the Suzuki would have a top speed of ninety miles an hour.

'Forty, my god that's faster than some trains, that's amazing, awh, crikey here comes the lorry, Harry I'd love to have another go on that thing can I?'

'Certainly as soon as we get back to Raven-Scar,' replied Harry. The lorry laboured up the hill and stopped about a hundred yards from the waiting group; the driver walked over to them asking what was to go, and he had been told that Harry and Tina would follow on the machine. The lorry was soon loaded Tina's bike being the last item to be loaded it would be dropped off at raven-Scar. And with Henson and the driver onboard it set off back down the hill through Harwood Dale and onto Raven-Scar, Tina wanted a word with Harry she knew he was thinking of another hair brained idea.

'What!' said Harry as he looked at Tina he knew that expression, 'What, have I done now?'

'I want to know what it is you're thinking of doing. If it's risky then forget it, just let's get back to Raven-Scar and see if we can speak to Lawson, Harry!' Her voice carried a threat. 'We have to ask him how he comes and goes so do not, and I mean it do not, make a mess of things.'

'Tina listen to me, we can get back to Raven-Scar on the Suzuki. See if we can speak to Lawson and get him to tell us how and where the 'thing' is then ride the bike back into Scarborough.'

'As simple as that is it? What happens if Lawson won't tell us anything unless we promise to take him back with us? He won't want to stay here with the risk of being hanged for murder and if he is in jail, which is highly likely under the circumstances, what then? We'll be stuck here. If they hang him and we don't get the chance to speak to him then we'll be stuck here. I don't think I would like that Harry.'

'No nor would I but if we do find where Lawson is, and I would think the Police would take him to Whitby, then well I don't know? Probably York, at least I take it that there is a Crown Court there in 1909. Anyway we find out from Lawson and if he refuses unless we do take him, well I suppose we shall have to take him as well. Mind you we don't know how injured he is, if he's been shot in the leg then he won't be able to move. I don't know about you but I think he should stay here and be punished for what he's done. It's not right to just kill someone, even though you're stealing from them; no I'm sorry Tina but if I can trick Lawson somehow I'll do it and let him remain here.'

The thought had occurred to Harry about what Lawson had said about the Suzuki running out of petrol; it would be a fairly easy task to siphon petrol out of the Army lorry's tank. Also, how would anybody know when that peculiar time warp would appear; it wasn't as if it could be switched on like a light. This 'thing' arrived by chance and maybe that it would suddenly disappear forever leaving people trapped.

Harry wondered how many other people were experiencing this phenomenon. Was it only the four that he knew of? Had it just appeared at this time purely by chance and then it would become no more, and if so it was imperative that he and Tina should be there whenever the opportunity arose for that cold dry dense mist to make an appearance. They needed to be able to pass through it back into their own time. Tina was thinking on the same lines as Harry and she voiced her thoughts to him. They agreed that Lawson, for whatever reason, had to remain in 1909 and accept the consequences of his wrong doings. But he would have to think that she and Harry would somehow take him with them; would the Suzuki carry three people? It would have to if Lawson couldn't walk.

Raven-Scar or the town that never was

Now they had to follow the lorry back to Raven-Scar and take things from there. The bike made swift progress along the muddy and rutted roads, sliding round corners with Tina holding on as the bike slewed left and right, until they reached the main road to Whitby. From there the road to Raven-Scar was as good as the main road and far better than the roads near Silpho Top. It gave them little problems. They arrived cold and grubby after the journey and propping the motor-bicycle against the Police station wall, they went inside to find Cyril and Agnes listening to the telephone. Cyril looked at the dishevelled pair and spoke into the phone.

'They have just arrived Sir,,, yes I can do that,,,, They seem to be alright,,,,Oh they went back to Scarborough half an hour ago, the Colonel will telephone you when the Sergeant has given him all the details. How is the robber? Lawson I mean,,,, Right then he shall be transferred on Thursday. Mmm, that doesn't give us much time to prepare our evidence does it? I shall have to go back through the record to find out details of the jewellers,,, Yes I can do that but what about the two banks, have we got enough evidence and more to the point what about witnesses?,,,,Oh I see yes that will be alright, I'll send it as soon as I write it up, say on the next train it gets here at three thirty so you should have it by quarter past four,,,
Thank you sir I'll do my best, good bye sir.' He replaced the ear piece into its cradle and placed the heavy black telephone back onto the counter.

'That was Detective Woods, let me see to-day is Tuesday, Lawson will be transferred on Thursday. I shall have to write up the report and get it on the train. You two look as if you have been dragged through a hedge backwards, I suggest you get a good wash and change those clothes.'

'What's happened to Lawson Cyril?' asked Harry.

'He's in Whitby jail waiting to go to the hospital to have his leg seen to, quite nasty it is too. The doctor who saw him here thinks that the bullet has shattered the bone and the leg may have to be amputated.'

'What, oh no that can't happen, if he has his leg amputated then we will have no chance of him helping us to find our way back. We have to see him as soon as possible, we have to or else we will be stuck here in your time, why did the soldiers have to shoot him?'

'Because he shot one of their men, the soldier tried to stop Lawson from riding that bike of yours down the road and Lawson shot him, not badly, but bad enough, so one of the snipers shot Lawson through the leg. That stopped him alright; we can't have killers running around with shotguns can us?' Cyril had a fair point.

'But we were hoping to get him to explain to us how and where he finds it possible to be able to find that weird mist, we realise that, that is the key. That mist is the sort of time slip and we have to find out where it starts from or is it random; we don't even know if it will appear again. But talking to Lawson we think it has something to do with the rail tunnel and it emanates from there, we think. Lawson told us he didn't know how to get back to his time but we think he was lying to us. He also told us that he thinks that our mobile phones trigger off the 'phenomena' if you like to call it that. Besides he was going to do another bank robbery.' Cyril was intrigued by Harry saying that Lawson was going to rob another bank.

'Was he now well he won't do that anymore? If he's found guilty then he will hang and that is the only correct sentence for any murderer don't you think?'

Raven-Scar or the town that never was

CHAPTER 20

That was a very difficult question to ask of two people who came from an age where capital punishment was a thing of the past. Even though Harry said that Lawson should face the consequences of what he had done, it still made him shudder at the thought of the hangman.

Here in this alternate world, the taking of one person's life was viewed with very grave concern and so the law was such that a life sentence was not enough for this crime. It made Harry and Tina uncomfortable to think that the man who had sheltered them on the moors, would forfeit his life for his crime. As he had said to them both, that he had not meant to do what he did, nonetheless the bank manager had paid with his life.

Harry had other things on his mind at this time, how to siphon petrol out of the Army lorry. That went down like a lead balloon, fat chance of that unless he rode the Suzuki to Scarborough. His idea was a no, no; he had to find another source of petrol. What about the taxi? That was it, he could take petrol from the taxi he hoped, it sounded good to him and he would confide in Tina.

Agnes said it was about time they all had something to eat, she went into her kitchen and a few minute later called them in; on the table was a pile of beef sandwiches and more mugs of tea, with buttered scones and jam.

Tina and Harry were famished; they had not eaten since the soldiers had given them breakfast early that morning at six thirty and they could hear their stomachs beginning to rumble. Harry piled into the large stack of sandwiches, but Tina took her time and ate slowly.

'Cyril when is Lawson to be taken to Leeds? Will they take him to Scarborough first?'

'Erm, no not really Tina, the train will take him to Malton then to Leeds. He may have to stay for a few days in York jail until evidence is taken and the witnesses contacted. The trial won't be immediate, mainly because of having to get witnesses to the court, from Guisborough and Whitby, and of course Mr Marlow the jeweller, as well as you two.

You will be the main witness for the prosecution and you will have to convince the jury that Lawson is not from this time; now that is going to be extremely difficult don't you think? If you stand up in the witness box and say what you know and the theory of. What was it? Einstein's theory of relativity, and let me say that if I did not believe how you came here, then I would say it was absolutely nonsense and the case against Lawson would collapse. Let me say now that no one will believe that story.'

'Do you really think we came from the future Cyril?'

'For what it's worth Tina yes I do; you can probably explain it better than I can, but both Agnes and I firmly believe that you two are not from this time.'

Agnes agreed with her husband. Science was an unknown quantity in 1909, the world of scientific discovery was just beginning to reach the imagination of the public. Fiction writers had found a new medium. First it was detective stories with Sherlock Holmes which were being read by a large number of people who really believed he existed. The motor car was still an oddity, railways covered the country, and wars would have accelerated science: the discovery of TNT by Nobel was an example. Science would leap ahead in the next few years. What this world would be like in 1914 was anyone's guess. In Harry and Tina's world that date was infamous as the start of WW1 and maybe this world would be better at settling grievances.

'I don't know about you three but may I make a suggestion?' Agnes was thinking about the trial of a man who as far as she and her husband were concerned, did not exist. He did exist of course, but to prove he did not exist in this 1909 was going to be impossible to convince people otherwise. So she had a suggestion simple as it was it could work. 'Tina and Harry want to find out how to return back to their time yes?' They all agreed on that. 'Good then what would happen if you did not turn up at the trial? No bear with me for a moment,' Agnes said as they stared at her. ' What I want to say is that if you two found out from Lawson how he comes and goes, then you two could just simply vanish and leave Lawson to face the music.' It was a simple idea.

'But if Lawson won't tell us unless we take him then there will be no trial? And a murderer would go free?' Harry was correct of course but Agnes was not to be outdone.

'Yes I know that but let's say that Cyril could persuade Detective Woods to keep Lawson here for even one night, then it may be possible to get him to tell you what you want to know. Promise him you will take him with you. Then let's say just before you get to this strange misty stuff, you have something wrong with the motorbike and you have to stop to find out what's wrong. We know, there's nothing wrong with it. He won't know that would he? You could get back on the motor bike and ride into the mist, leaving him here to face the trial. If his leg is broken, he won't be able to chase after you will he? And Cyril would recapture him and if he did that he may be made up to sergeant. What do you think?'

Cyril liked the idea of being a sergeant but he saw a flaw in the plan.

'Detective Woods said that Lawson would be put on the train to Malton then York, so how do we persuade Woods to leave him here for one night?'

'I've thought of that; if we say Marlow wants to look more closely at Lawson but can't get to Whitby for some reason. Say he's ill or too busy to travel. But Marlow is prepared to identify him if he brought Lawson to come here, then Woods would have no choice but to bring him here for one night. Then he could get the train to Scarborough in the morning and connect to York and Leeds from there. If I remember from your training manual Cyril, a witness has to be given every opportunity to identify a suspect even if it means that suspect has to travel. I know Marlow would jump at the chance, just tell him that the publicity in the newspaper would be good for business if he did as we suggest. Then tell him that it would be easier for him to make a positive identity of Lawson if that man was here overnight.'

Agnes was pleased with her idea and so were the two time travellers. It could work. It all depended of course if that strange dry, cold mist would oblige them by being where they wanted it and that was no guarantee. Neither was there any guarantee that Lawson would cooperate, but if things were explained to him that this was his only chance of not being hanged, then he would be a fool not to agree. Detective Woods could also be disinclined to bring his prisoner to Raven-Scar on some trumped-up excuse concerning the rights of a witness. Naturally it was such a simple plan, so much so that it could work. Time as is said to 'sleep on it'.

CHAPTER 21

Tina wanted to talk to Harry. She would have to creep downstairs and talk to him in his 'cell'. She always thought this amusing, finding Harry in his 'cell'. Cyril was in conversation with his wife, Tina heard him say that he would telephone the Sergeant in the morning and try to persuade him to bring Lawson to Raven-Scar. Cyril left the Police Station house to ask Mr Marlow if he would agree to a little scheme he had prepared, Tina and Harry retired to their respective rooms for the night. Tina heard Cyril return and the faint mumble of voices in the kitchen, then Mr and Mrs Whitaker aka Constable Whitaker climbed the stairs to their room.

Tina waited until she was sure they were asleep, creeping down the cold stairs she tiptoed into the station office, regretting that she had not put on her trainers: the stone slabs on the office floor made her shudder. She whispered to Harry. 'Are you asleep?'

'No come on in we have to talk. Sit down on the edge of this bunk, careful its blooming hard.' Tina sat down next to him as Harry draped a blanket over them to keep warm Tina shivered with cold.

'That's better, thanks Harry, listen do you think Agnes's idea will work?'

'It will, if Cyril can persuade Detective Woods to bring Lawson here.'

'And if not, what happens then?' Tina was desperate to have an answer; this world was not the one she wanted to be left in, to live a strange life. She wanted to be with her family and friends. She thought this was not too much to ask, their hopes rested with Lawson.

'I have no idea Tina; I suppose we will just have to hope that we can somehow find out where that time gap is. Let's not think like that let's think positively; we have to or else we'll lose any hope. Now what I have to do before it gets light is find out where one of the taxis is kept. I thought I saw one of them standing in that garage in the main road, I don't recall seeing a petrol pump there did you?'

'Yes I did? Harry I forgot to tell you there is a pump there but it's one of those old fashioned ones where you have to pump it with a handle. You can't see it from the road it's tucked away behind the garage under a sort of awning thing; it must belong to the taxi owner.' Harry laughed at his companion's remark about an old fashioned item, saying it should be old fashioned it was one hundred years old. Tina grinned at him she realised what she had said. 'Do you think you can manage to use the pump?'

'I think so it's just a case of holding the pump nozzle into the tank and pulling the handle: you'll have to help me though I can't hold and pump at the same time. What time is it now? Let me see, it's nine thirty; if I wake you at five in the morning we should be able to push the bike to the garage. Fortunately it's slightly downhill. I suppose we shall have to push it until we can start it up so as not to waken whoever sleeps at the garage'.

Tina and Harry stood shivering in the cold misty dark in the garage forecourt. The one pump stood like a sentinel, the six-foot tall square metal object with its glass 'Shell' logo on the top stood like a soldier on guard. The pump handle pointed upright like a rifle, the nozzle hanging from it's cradle on the left, both children shivered with the cold. It seemed as if Raven-Scar was blessed with an inordinate amount of 'sea-fret'. Probably in their time that was one of the reasons why nothing was ever done about turning this bleak place into a town, but in this time and century it had been built. As far as they could tell it was a thriving place with its one petrol pump, bank, a goodly number of shops

Raven-Scar or the town that never was

selling anything from jewellery to ice-cream: not that Tina and Harry wanted ice-cream this time in the morning, all they wanted was in this silent obelisk.

It was dark at this time and the meagre shelter over the pump provided some small place to hide their nefarious deed, that of stealing. Harry stood the Suzuki on its side stand as near as he could get to the side of the pump he unhooked the nozzle from its cradle and whispered to Tina.

'Hold this into the tank Tina while I pump the handle; tell me when it's full?'

'I can't see into the tank Harry it's too dark, I'll tell you when I think it's nearly full; go ahead and pump and let's get out of here. Harry grasped the black ball on top on the pump handle and pulled downwards.

'It's not moving Tina I can't pull it down there must be a knack to using these old pumps. I think you'll have to help me with it, leave the bike and give me a hand: if the tank overflows then it's tough luck as long as we get petrol into it, I don't care come on quickly.' Tina lent her weight on the handle and suddenly the metal rod moved down and they could hear the gurgling of petrol slopping into the bikes tank. The rod shot back upright before they could stop it and the noise it made, made them both jump back startled.

'Shhh' hissed Tina.

'I am shhhing! It's the handle, I didn't expect t to be that strong; oh crikey there's a light in that house over there, get down.' They both ducked behind the petrol pump as the door in the house opened and a figure of a short stocky man appeared. His attire was strange by Tina and Harry's standards as he was dressed in oil skins with his head covered in a sloping yellow hat covering his neck and shoulders. The figure waited until a slightly smaller figure appeared in the open doorway and both figures kissed goodbye. The fisherman walked swiftly toward Raven-Scar harbour, his daily toil would begin when his boat was pushed into the sea and rowed further out until its one sail could be raised.

'Phew that was close! I was sure they had heard the noise; let me see if I can tell how much is in the tank?' Harry poked his finger into the bikes tank he sniffed the end of it as he withdrew it, 'another pull Tina and we should just about fill it' he whispered. Both pulled down on the handle but this time they clung on until the handle had returned to its upright position. Harry poked his finger once more into the petrol tank. 'It's full to the top. I wonder how much the pump dispenses at one go, it must be a lot?'

'Who cares how much it puts out? Let's get out of this place it's beginning to get light.' Tina sounded agitated so they began to push the motor-bicycle off its stand and up the slightly sloping hill of the main road. 'Just a minute Harry, let's have a rest, my arms ache: it's heavier than it looks. Can you start it up do you think? At least we can ride it back to near Cyril's house.'

Harry turned the ignition key, thumbed the starter button and the Suzuki burbled into life. Harry found it difficult to mount the bike, as it stood tall on its suspension, but once in the saddle the bike settled down. Tina hitched up her voluminous skirt and clambered onto the pillion seat, grabbing hold of Harry's waist; she clung on as Harry put the bike into gear and pulled away.

He daren't put the headlight on as anybody out and about would notice a bright yellow bike: also the street lights were not very good being gas and showing a shadowy yellow glow, as they rode slowly up towards the Police Station house. Harry remembered the story of 'Jack the Ripper' who terrorised London in the later part of the nineteenth century. The gloomy street lighting threw shadows which made one's imagination think of a doom laden atmosphere; he shivered but not from the cold, more from his thoughts.

They now had another problem. Where to put the motor-bicycle so that they could easily make a getaway? It would not be the best thing to do to keep it too near the Police Station: also by now it was light enough to make out the road that made its way to the level crossing, over the

Raven-Scar or the town that never was

road, before the railway ran into the tunnel. Harry turned the bike towards this road and Tina asked where he was going? Harry did not answer: he knew where he was going, into the tunnel. They went inside and Harry switched on the Suzuki's lights and the beam showed up the inside of the tunnel. The walls were sooty from the smoke of the trains; he noticed there were 'cut-outs' in the side of the structure.

'We'll leave the bike in one of those places.'

'What are they for Harry? Are they for people to stand in when a train comes, if they are why would people be in the tunnel anyway?'

'Oh, I remember reading about railway tunnels; my dad has a book on tunnels, don't ask, you're right they are for men to get into. The maintenance men would work in tunnels, making sure that the lines would be sound and I suppose they would inspect the tunnel's brickwork for cracks and such like. Men were employed by the rail companies to walk along the lines making sure all was correct: one or two of the old track side maintenance huts still stand on the old line you know, have you never noticed them when we are riding along?'

'Oh, is that what they are for I never knew that I thought they were just well, little huts I never gave them much thought; but just a minute if we leave the bike in one of those cut outs someone will be bound to notice it, I mean you can't but not notice a bright yellow motor bike can you. Besides it's not something that's seen every day is it not like in our time if someone does find it they would immediately tell the Police surely.'

'Yes I suppose you're right the only thing we can do is hide it under something. I think that I noticed a tarpaulin when we entered the tunnel come on let's get it and cover it up.' The 'tarp' just covered the bike, and using a couple of planks, that the maintenance men had left lying about, the bike was more or less covered up. Which was just as well as they could hear the early morning train blowing its whistle as it came into Raven-Scar station. This would be the mail, and milk train. It would stop for about ten minutes, or should have done, but this train did not stop it came straight into the tunnel puffing and steaming filling the void with smoke and steam. In the gloom of the tunnel, the light from the fire box showed the faces of Albert and Jack, the two train drivers they had met in the café, a long time ago it seemed to them, Jack was leaning out of the cab as the train thundered towards the two children.

Harry dragged Tina into one of the cut outs as the train charged through the blackness. They clung to each other as it sped past them, showering them with soot and cinders. They cowered into the brick wall as the train dragging its load went past, the guards van clattered past and the tunnel became calm and quiet, once more.

'That was close.' Harry stood holding Tina. They both smelt of soot and smoke and Harry could make out Tina's face, white as a sheet with bits of black soot peppering her face. With her eyes wide open, unable to speak, he held her close until she said in a trembling voice.

'I think after this Harry I don't want to go into another tunnel as long as I live. I was very scared I thought we would be killed. Why didn't it stop like it usually did? Oh, Harry do you think it would be going to Whitby to bring Lawson back here? I'll bet that's why it didn't stop. Cyril must have persuaded the Detective to bring Lawson here, that's why it didn't stop, it had to get to Whitby in time to bring him to Raven-Scar for him to be identified. Harry I'll bet that's it don't you think so?'

The question hung in the air as Harry released Tina from his grasp. He had held her tight because he too was terrified of the train, but being a boy he felt he could not show fear; they were both very near to the edge of their nerves and the sooner they could get to ask the vital question the sooner they could return to 2009.

CHAPTER 22

PC Whitaker met the two early birds on the road leading into town.

'Ah, there you are what are you doing at this time in the morning?'

'We er, decided to go for a walk. we couldn't sleep, what with all the excitement yesterday. Cyril did you manage to persuade detective Woods to bring Lawson here?' Tina asked him.

'Well yes and no that is Lawson will be coming, but will not be staying long, just long enough for Mr Marlow to identify him. Mr Woods was quite adamant on that. I'm sorry but it was all I could do to persuade Woods to bring him; he was furious about it, he said I should have taken Mr Marlow to Whitby yesterday, until I explained that Mr Marlow was ill and could not take the train. Mr Marlow does not know why we asked him and I don't want him to know, so keep this to ourselves OK, or else I'll be dismissed from the force. Anyhow, I've given some thought to the situation and I've had a word with Agnes. Do you know I never thought my wife could be so devious, good job she's married to a copper or else I'll be chasing her for some misdeed or other,' he chuckled at his thoughts. 'Listen to this though; we've thought of a way to delay Lawson overnight which should give us a chance to extract any information from him. Agnes reckons that if we give Lawson some food, say a sandwich or soup, she knows a herb that can make a person feel ill for a few hours, not enough to make them incapacitated, but ill enough to be not moved; a bit like senna-pods do. If we can do that then you could speak to Lawson and get him to tell you where and what to look out for. I must admit it's a long shot, this idea of Lawson telling you anything, he's a pretty hard case you know, it takes a certain person to shoot at anyone, so what do you think?.'

Cyril turned round at the sound of someone calling him, 'Hello what does he want?' The person concerned was a tall man wearing a brown overall and a scruffy flat cap with bits of grey hair sticking out from under it.

'Constable I'm glad I've caught you before your rounds', the man was slightly short of breath.

'Yes Mr Johnston what's the problem?'

'Stealing Constable, that's what the problem is, stealing petrol, there's only three cars and the two taxi's in Raven-Scar, aye there's the charabanc of course but I'd 'ave 'erd 'im certainly'

'How do you know that someone has taken petrol Mr Johnston?'

'I take a measure evenings and mornings to see 'ow much I've got in the tank does see, and this morn does not tally wi' what I took last neet. It's only say a gallon but I can tell it's gone; it must 'ave been teken before Amos went to his boat. I've asked his wife if they saw 'owt and she says no. It's a bit of a mystery Constable but I'm very sure it's gone.'

'Harry did either of you see anything unusual when you were out early this morning?' Cyril eyed the two unwilling time travellers.

'No not a thing Mr Whitaker' Harry said. 'Anyway how much is a gallon of petrol?'

'One shilling and tuppence' replied Mr Johnston. 'Why?'

'Oh just curious that's all' Harry would pay Mr Johnston for a gallon of petrol but he was not going to say he and Tina had filled up the motor-bicycles petrol tank.

'Mr Johnston if you come with me back to the Station we can fill out a report, then we can ask around also we can make enquiries with the vehicle owners.'

Raven-Scar or the town that never was

'Nay Constable I don't want to do that, those people are my customers and they won't take kindly to me accusing them of stealing.'

'Then what do you want me to do Mr Johnston? You can make a charge to person or persons unknown, or take the loss of a gallon of petrol, it's up to you. I can do my duty but as you say the people who own motor vehicles are your customers. Shall I make out a report?'

'Nay Constable if you put it like that I'll not make a charge this time but I'll mek damn sure nobody can use my pump wi'out my knowledge I can tell thee. I'll put a lock on it, and to think someone in this town can stoop so low as to steal from a petrol pump, but I'll tell thee this Constable, there must be another vehicle in this town that I know n'owt about. Anyroad I thought I'd mention it just to make sure you know what's 'appened. I'll say no more now but I'll 'ave a discrete word meself like. Good-bye Constable, I'll probably see thee in Horse and Wagon, G'morning.' Mr Johnston turned round and walked back down the hill to the garage.

'Are you sure you know nothing of this?' asked Cyril.

'No nothing we just went for a walk as we told you' said Tina holding her breath, Cyril nodded.

'Well that's not important: what's more important now is how we get Lawson to divulge how he can come and go through time. And something that puzzles me is, why has no one else slipped through this time gap? As far as I know only you three, and of course the hiker Mr Broadbent, are the only ones to arrive this way. Have you any clues; did Lawson say anything that could be useful? Think about it, anything at all?'

'The only thing he said when we spoke to him in the field barn was that he went through a very cold, dark, very dry mist. What Mr Lawson did say and its something that is a possibility was that somehow that the computer chips in our mobile phones may, just may, have something to do with it. And when we think back to how we went into the café near the station, that was what we felt wasn't it Tina, a very cold dry mist?'

'Yes I said to Harry that it was getting very cold and I would like a hot drink before we rode back to Scarborough. Ha!, That was wishful thinking on my part. We are stuck here in your time and we are no further on to finding how to return. We may have to live with you Cyril if we can't go back or forward. I suppose we have to say that. Can a policeman adopt time travellers?' Tina found this funny in a way, so did Cyril, Harry looked at Tina aghast.

'Don't think like that, we'll go back oh, alright then forward. Tina you are annoying, you are confusing me, are we going back? Or are we going into the future? That's if we can of course.'

'Into the future of course, I hope not into this future but in our time. Harry I've had a thought, if we find this mysterious misty stuff what happens if we walk into it? Will we be projected backwards like we have been, or do we walk into it backwards and hope we are projected forwards?' Harry and Cyril looked at Tina for a few moments, and then looked at each other, and then back to Tina, Harry had never given any thought as to how they should enter the freezing mist; would it make any difference? Cyril pondered the question Tina had raised a valid point and it might be that the way to move in time was the way one entered this strange mist. All the people so far had walked into the mist, even Lawson must have done this, then how did he get back to his own time, did he walk backwards? No, that was too silly an idea. Tina was just thinking up ideas to keep herself from feeling dispirited, but she may have a point, the only way was to get to Lawson. Cyril suddenly gave a start.

'It's the tunnel, Tina and Harry that's the location, the tunnel there has to be something in the tunnel that turns time, think about it, Lawson goes into the tunnel and comes out in a different time, same as Broadbent. He was coming out of the tunnel and you two were not very far from it when you went into the café. The tunnel is only a hundred yards from the station.'

'But the train that stopped not long after we went into the café, that didn't vanish did it?' Tina made that very plain, which took the wind out of Cyril's sails for the moment.

'Yes that's right but didn't Lawson say that the mist went as quickly as it came and he mentioned our mobiles? I'm sure he said that when he spoke to us; we must remember what to say to him and if he won't cooperate what then? How can we get him out of his cell? I presume he will be in a cell even if he is ill, will he Cyril?'

'Most certainly he will Harry.'

'Well I think that the idea to make him ill, is the only chance we will have to speak to him, then if he doesn't tell us anything unless we take him we shall have to get him out of the cell and walk him to the tunnel somehow Harry can we get three on the bike without falling off? Oh! What am I saying we don't even know if this mist will be there do we? If it isn't and we take Lawson out of jail we'll face charges of aiding and abetting a criminal to escape and we'll be put in jail. I don't fancy that do you Harry? It's all ifs and buts isn't it? Am I being defeatist do you think? My mind is thinking all sorts of things that could go wrong or not even happen, then we'll be in trouble, double trouble.' Tina was logical as usual.

The 11-15am train from Whitby steamed into Raven-Scar; the prisoner was under the care of Detective Woods and one other constable, he had a chain round his good leg, which was attached to the constable's waist and the Detective was armed with a standard police issue Webley .32 revolver. Detective Woods was taking no chances with Lawson. That man however was not going to get very far with or without his chain. He had to support himself on two wooden crutches and hobbled along on these. From the train station to the Police Station was a slow progression. Lawson's face was drawn and haggard. He had a bruise over his left eye, which was the aftermath of his capture by the soldiers, who had meted out their own punishment on a man who had the audacity to shoot one of their men.

By the time the three men had reached the Police Station the prisoner was needing support. He was helped into the office, where he collapsed exhausted onto a chair. He certainly didn't look like the 'hard man' that Harry and Tina had met in the field barn. Now he hung his head, bowed low with the pain from his wound. He was placed in the second cell and left there whilst the three Policemen gathered in the office.

'How's Lawson?' asked PC Cyril Whitaker.

'The Doctor reckons his leg will heal. Also I've had words with the Leeds Chief Constable about him. He's of the opinion that after treatment at St James', where they will patch him up sort of, his trial will be very quickly dealt with and if the verdict is as we think, he will be transferred to Armley Jail. That's where he will be hanged when the judge decides on the time and date. I have to say that this is an unusual case constable and it shall be dealt with as swiftly as possible.'

'I agree, now if you don't mind I'll go and chivvy up Mr Marlow, he did say he would get here by, 3pm.

'What!' exploded Detective Woods? 'Come on constable, I want to be away before then. This man has to be kept overnight in York and then transferred to Leeds. It's a devil of a job taking prisoners by train. We don't know if this man has any accomplices who can make an attempt to free him.'

'Hardly sir when you remember where he came from, the same place and time as Tina and Harry, from the future?'

'That's as may be. I still have reservations on that constable and until this case is over I find it very hard to believe what I have seen and heard. Nonetheless I still will be glad when it's all over. By the way how are those two youngsters doing?'

Raven-Scar or the town that never was

Those two youngsters had been listening to the conversation with growing alarm; if Lawson was to leave as soon as possible, then there would be no opportunity to ask him anything. Harry ushered Tina out of the room.

'We have to get to Agnes and tell her to make sure Lawson becomes too ill to travel to-day. Let's have a word with her'. Harry guided Tina into the kitchen where Agnes was setting a tray with mugs and a pot of tea and biscuits. When she saw them enter the kitchen she smiled.

'Do you know I think the Police Force runs on tea and biscuits?'

'Agnes we must speak to you, please it's urgent' Tina took the tray of biscuits while Agnes pushed the door open and went into the office. When she returned she settled into her chair.

'Right loves I think I can do what has to be done, have either of you heard of Senna pods?'

'No what are they? Harry thought he recognised the words but wasn't too sure of what they were.

'It's an old fashioned remedy for, well you know going to the toilet if you're bunged up like.'

'Oh I see, you mean like if you have constipation? Tina thought it sounded amusing to be thinking of that at a time like this.

'Aye that's right. Bunged up like: listen keep your voices down they can 'ere in the office you know. So what I propose to do is, make up a potion and add it to some vegetable soup I made this morning. Cyril does like his veggie soup.'

'But if you put it in the soup we will all be, you know, going.'

'Nay Tina I'm not as daft as to do that, I'll just put it in Mr Lawson's soup. Believe you me once he gets this down him he'll be lucky if he can leave here in the morning.' Agnes had a slightly revengeful streak in her makeup. Lawson would find life a bit hectic during the night.

CHAPTER 23

The dirty deed was done. Lawson had his soup before Mr Marlow saw him. That man said he was definitely the one who had robbed him of a huge amount of jewellery. The amount and value was erm! Increasing all the time. Mr Marlow showed all the instincts of a grasping man and saw the opportunity of getting the better of his insurance company. He had told PC Whitaker that more items had been stolen than originally he had thought. All this was written down and would be sent to the insurance company for them to either dispute the claim or pay out the money. But with the impending court case, Mr Marlow felt confident that the insurance would pay out, the publicity would be good for all concerned. It was not too long before Lawson complained of stomach pains and had to be escorted to the toilet. Harry and Tina saw their opportunity; taking a glass of water to the cell Harry whispered to the inmate.

'Mr Lawson, we have to know how you can go back and forth through time, how do you do it. We have to know we have to get back to our own time; will you tell us what you know and how we can find out where it is?'

Lawson drank from the glass proffered by Harry. He limped back to his bed in the cell, holding his stomach and he doubled up in pain.

'Got to think, Harry isn't it?' Harry affirmed that was his name. 'Listen I don't know how I can help, oh these pains, call someone I've got to go again.' Tina called for Detective Woods, who half carried Lawson to the out-side toilet. There happened to be no flush toilets in the row of houses, the loo's were in the outbuildings at the rear of the premise.

Raven-Scar or the town that never was

Lawson limped back in and was locked up in his cell. Detective Woods had a conference with PC Whitaker.

'Damn it Constable, I can't take him on the train as he is; there must have been something in the soup. Do you feel alright? I must say I enjoyed mine and don't feel untoward. Do you?'

'Not in the least. My Agnes knows how to cook and I can't think why Lawson has stomach upset,' although he had a very good idea and hoped the ruse would work.

'I'll have to telephone York and say that Lawson and his escort can't make it at the appropriate time. This won't go down well with the magistrate, I had a word with him t'other day about this case and he states that he will refer it to the Crown Court in Leeds. Curses, this throws everything into a panic; now the courts will have to reconvene at a later date.' Entering the station office, he took up the telephone and dialled the operator; Cyril closed the door and went into the kitchen.

'By 'eck lass how much stuff did you put into Lawson's soup? It's fair got him going. Mr Woods says he can't move him in this state, so where are those two youngsters?' Agnes told him they were in the cell block. Cyril hurried there to find Lawson wanting to go again. Helping the limping criminal once again to the outside loo, he returned on his own. 'Best leave him for a while until he erm, clears his self out. Has he told you anything important yet?'

'No nothing we just get talking, then whoosh, he has to go again.' PC Whitaker gave a low chuckle mainly to himself, but made sure Harry and Tina heard him.

'It's not funny Cyril, if Lawson can't move from here then he can't show us anything' Tina was not inclined to smile at the moment.

'Don't worry if I know Agnes she will have put just enough stuff into Lawson's soup to make him feel out of sorts for a few hours. Don't worry, by ten o clock tonight he'll be as right as rain you see. Then it's too late for the train: the last one through here is 9-30 p.m. so he's going nowhere. Are you certain he hasn't said anything?'

'No not a thing, well nothing that makes sense. Cyril has anything strange happened, such as something or somebody such as a train, suddenly disappearing?'

'I think we would have noticed a vanishing train young lady.'

'Cyril we are certain that the answer is in the tunnel from what we can make out from the little that Mr Lawson has said. Are you positive that nothing like that has occurred?'

'No Harry, I'm positive that nothing or no one has suddenly vanished. As for a train, well are you serious, a train indeed, never such nonse.... Crikey, come on, follow me. I've just remembered summat that's in the day book. Come on.' Cyril charged out of the cell room into the station office and took the daily report book from under the counter. He thumbed through the pages and let out a deep sigh.

'Yes I thought so,' turning the book round so that Harry and Tina could read what had been written. 'Quick read this before Detective Woods returns: he's gone to the rail station to make sure there is an early morning train. Look what's been recorded.'

"On this date, the 9.30am train to Whitby reported that stray animals were on the line outside Staintondale Station. Mr Adams, of Manor Farm Raven-Scar, was contacted, as this was the more likely place that the animals were from but he and one of his men scoured the line from Staintondale to here and reported that there were no animals on the line. Mr Adams did say that a number of his sheep had been stolen and told me, PC Whitaker, that the culprits were more than likely rustlers. One of his men had noticed a peculiar vehicle around the time of the sheep going missing. He also accused the train driver of malicious rumour. Both the driver and the fireman stated that what they saw was correct. Later the Station Masters of Staintondale and here at Raven-Scar sent a telephone

Raven-Scar or the town that never was

message stating that a number of sheep where moving along the line. The Station Master of Raven-scar reported that the animals came through his station running very quickly; they ran into the tunnel and he reported down the line for the down train to take care, as the tunnel has a slight curve in it and visibility is limited. The animals seem to have found their way back to Manor Farm, as no animals were reported by the down train driver. Signed PC Whitaker."

Harry looked at the Policeman with a puzzled look.

'How has this anything to do with Lawson? It's just a coincidence that the sheep strayed onto the line then found their own way back.'

'Aha, it could be, but look at the next page; the date is the following day, the day that Mr Marlow the jeweller was robbed. He and another witness mentioned a peculiar vehicle, a bit like a motor-cycle, carrying the robber away. Now all this may be a coincidence but I think that Lawson found himself back in time and the sheep found themselves changing places with him. They all must have hit the same spot at the same time, hence the sheep vanishing and Lawson turning up here. I must say he appears to be an opportunist, remember the dead man on the line Mr Broadbent. He met with a train. Now what we have to find out is what triggers this phenomenon, any ideas?'

Tina and Harry thought long and hard, but an answer to this puzzle eluded them. There had to be a trigger, something simple, that only happens when a certain something makes contact with whatever is in the tunnel or adjacent to it. But whatever it was, the answer could only come from one person and that person was still outside. If the answer was a simple trigger, like a mobile phone that Lawson had suggested, Harry was thinking on those lines.

'My goodness I'd forgotten Lawson is still outside, I hope he hasn't run off?' Then Cyril grinned. 'Probably not with his leg like it is; besides he's only got one leg in his trousers, the doctor at Whitby hospital cut it off so that he could attend to Lawson's wound.'

Lawson, bank robber and murderer was still sitting in the outside loo with a pained expression on his face.

'It must be something I've eaten; there must have been something in that soup, why aren't any of you affected?' Cyril said nothing and Harry thought you would not like to know what was in your soup. Tina thought, poor man not only is he in pain from his leg but in pain from his stomach. Still he was a criminal and he had killed someone.

When they had managed to get Lawson back into his cell he asked for something to drink so Cyril went into the kitchen where Agnes brewed more tea. She reminded her husband that the time was very late and that the Detective would return very soon, so it was imperative that information was gathered from Lawson. Cyril agreed with her and returned to the cell with tea and biscuits. Agnes was correct; the Police Force relied on a steady intake of tea and biscuits to perform their duties. Setting the tray down and pouring out the tea Cyril asked the question.

'Mr Lawson you are in serious trouble and when found guilty, not if, when, you will be hanged so listen to me. These two young'uns want to return to theirs and your time, and they can only do that with your help. You seem to be able to come and go sort of and what we want to know is how and where? Is there some form of invisible doorway type of thing or what? We have a plan to get you out of here. Against my better judgment mind you because it may mean I would be in serious trouble with my superiors, if you suddenly disappear. That is the plan, simply that you disappear. You will take these two on the motor bike to the place that you know of and then return into your future, but only if you cooperate fully, do you understand?'

'Yes I understand but you're a copper, and in my experience coppers don't strike bargains with the likes of me, so what's in it for you, I mean I can take these two back if the time is right and the 'thing' is there?'

Raven-Scar or the town that never was

'Thing, what thing, you mean that there is something that you can pass through, like that very cold, dark mist that we occasionally find'?' asked Tina.

'Yes exactly. My god this tea is just the job I must say, I'm feeling a hell of a lot better than I did earlier. What time is it, they took my watch away in Whitby?'

'It's ten to eleven and if you have anything to say better say it now before the Detective comes back, then we can work some form of plan out.' Cyril was keen to know how this phenomenon really did work and if he was there when it happened; he would write a novel about time travel, much better than what H G Wells had ever written.

The phone in the office rang they could hear Agnes speaking then she shouted out to Cyril, 'love those two detectives are stayin' at the hotel Mr Woods says he will be here at 8p.m. I'm going to bed love goodnight.' Her footsteps echoed up the stairs as she climbed them to her bedroom.

Lawson leaned back on the bunk bed fastened to the cell wall.

'Harry lad lift my leg up onto the bunk please, it hurts a lot when it's down, thanks lad, that's better. Now I can tell you how I found out about this 'thing'. That's what I'll call it, for want of anything else. About a year ago my mates and I were.... Constable if I tell you everything what will happen to me? I mean will I get a lighter sentence or something? I see, ok then here goes.' Cyril had shaken his head in answer to Lawson's question. 'As I was saying I and some of my mates were up on the moors with a large animal transporter. We had around forty sheep rounded up and getting them into the van, when a helicopter suddenly appeared from nowhere. We were about ready to go and this thing came up; my mates legged it out of the van and ran straight into the arms of half a dozen Policemen. I scarpered on my bike down toward the old rail track. In the dark it was a bit hairy like, but I found a lane which took me onto the track and I headed in the wrong direction towards Ravenscar instead of Scarborough. I knew I was wrong when I went past the old station and then I ran headlong into the tunnel. I knew it was blocked up and there was no way through, so I panicked I can tell you and tried to turn around; it was very dark, misty and very cold. The headlight showed up the blocked exit and I nearly ran into it, only I didn't, I came out of the tunnel the other end onto the railway lines, I couldn't believe it. I turned round and went back into the tunnel and saw that the lines carried on. Then I arrived at the station. I was gobsmacked; there just should not have been neither a station nor any lines, so what the heck was happening. At first I thought I had stumbled onto the filming of Heart-Beat or something like that…'

'Yes that's what we thought when we went into the café' said Tina.

'Yes well how do you think I felt, I had escaped from the Police only to run smack into a film set or so I thought. It was around two in the morning, so I rode back into the tunnel and, nothing, the mist and cold had gone. I felt very weird I can tell you; what was happening and what was I going to do? At this late time I decided to kip down somewhere, so I went into one of those little huts that they used to have alongside of the tracks, you know like a shelter, I hid my bike in some bushes and went to sleep. I woke up when I heard a train, I thought I was dreaming until I looked out the window and saw a train standing at the station and saw people dressed in clothing that was very old. It had to be a film set hadn't it? I thought, and then I crept out of the hut and went towards the station. People looked at me very strangely, as I was still dressed in my motor-cycle gear and carrying my helmet. Then I saw a Policeman looking at me and he started to walk towards me. I wasn't going to answer any questions, so I ran back to where I left my bike, fired it up and rode into the tunnel. I switched on the lights and ran into that freezing mist and the dark and nearly ran into the blocked end, I fell off the bike then. I was baffled and I have to confess a bit frightened: anyway I turned round and rode out of the

Raven-Scar or the town that never was

tunnel and found I was back in my own time; that's when I knew that I had been through a time slip or something.'

'Mr Lawson tell me one thing, does the dark mist only manifest itself in the tunnel?' Tina wanted to know.

'Manifest?, oh you mean only there; no is the answer, but it doesn't appear to move very far from the tunnel, at least that's what I have found. In the end I thought it was just a bit of fun to ride up here and suddenly be in another time. Aha, but let me tell you this, it, or the 'thing,' is not there all the time and for some reason it comes and goes and you have to be lucky if you find it. I did wonder how many people had been caught out with it and gone somewhere and not returned. I mean if you committed a robbery in say our time you could come here and disappear couldn't you?'

'You could if you knew the 'thing' was here but how do you know that it is?' Harry had a point and Mr Lawson answered him.

'You don't, that's the problem, and all I can tell you is that it seems to be adjacent to the tunnel here but does move along the old track. When I robbed the banks in Guisborough, and Whitby I only had to ride on the rail lines towards Raven-Scar and bingo I ran into it, fortunately for me. All right constable I admit it along with the others, but I didn't mean to harm anyone with the gun honestly, I used it to frighten people. Still I did kill the man and I regret that. But I had to ride to Whitby from Guisborough and then to Raven-Scar before I could have any chance of going back or forward if you like. But don't you see it was exciting to be able to do what I was doing? I mean committing crimes in one world and then returning to your own world was a dream come true to someone like me. I could get away Scot free and it was great. So I played along with this phenomenon for the better part of a year. Sometimes I was lucky, other times I had to hide away until I found that the 'thing' was there. Now I think about it, it has something to do with electrics.'

'How do you know that?' asked Tina.

'The first time it happened I told you I rode into the tunnel by mistake and it was dark and I had the headlight on the bike as I said. I nearly ran slap bang into the blockage, and then suddenly I was not, I mean running into the wall; the wall wasn't there when I came out of the mist but it didn't dawn on me until the second time. I'd pootled around the area and probably frightened some people when I appeared. I'd thought of finding a B&B in Raven-Scar, then realised my money and appearance would cause suspicion, so I slept rough. I had time to think things through, so I went back into the tunnel. Don't forget I was in this world in this time. Anyway back I went and by now it was getting dark so I took a torch, which I keep in the bike, and followed the rail tracks into the tunnel. I walked to the end and nothing, no mist nothing. I felt deflated, until I walked back and found that weird mist. By walking through it I came out in my own time. I used my mobile to contact one of my mates to find out what had happened.

He told me that the Police were preparing a charge of sheep rustling, so I thought stuff that I'm not going back yet. I turned round and walked back into this time. I turned round again, turned off the torch and walked back down the tunnel. Nothing, no mist at all, it had gone, but I walked out into this time, I tried to use my mobile, nothing as you've realised? Am I making sense about all this?'

'I suppose so, but if as you say, it has something to do with electrics then why is it that Harry and I came here we don't have anything electrical on us and what about the trains they have electrics on them don't they?'

Tina had a very valid point, and one that made Harry think quickly,

'Phones Tina we have phones which run on batteries, the same as Mr Broadbent, he had a phone and a camera and the trains I've seen here still have oil lamps even on the engines. They obviously run older trains on these branch lines, and nobody has disappeared in our time, well not to our knowledge they haven't, and Mr Lawson has told us that this 'thing' is not here all the time. Just supposing that it is a random phenomenon and moves itself through time and space and only occurs at very irregular intervals; that would explain a great deal wouldn't it?'

Lawson looked at Harry with interest, 'Do you know Harry I thought the same thing myself and felt that at some time I would be lost in one world or another, I think you're right. Listen, I promise you two that if we do get back to our time, I'll give myself up to the Police, not for murder, I can't say I killed someone in 1909 can I, but I'll say I've been rustling and so forth. Does that sound reasonable to you?'

'May be, but we still have to hope that the tunnel is the place where we can definitely enter the time zone. We don't know for sure do we?' That was the problem; was it the tunnel or not? Only one way to find out, and that was to get there ASAP.

CHAPTER 24

PC Whitaker had to be very careful, if the plan that had been arranged worked out like they planned. Lawson was in better shape than a few hours ago, he still could not walk very far without his crutches, and he was a condemned man. Lawson had committed murder and by rights he should face the consequences, but to get Tina and Harry back to their own time and Lawson's the plan had to work.

The problem of course was if they could, it would be a lost cause if the three of them managed to ride the Suzuki into Raven-Scar tunnel to find that the phenomena was absent That would be disastrous for all concerned, especially for him PC Whitaker. Not only would he loose his prisoner, he would most certainly lose his job and more than likely end up in Armley Jail. Time was marching on and Agnes had told him that Detective Woods and the constable were staying at one of the hotels in town and would take Lawson on the 10-20 a. m. train to Scarborough, then onto York. Cyril and the three time travellers had to try to get some sleep, wake early and find the way to return to their own time very quickly, before the Detective collected his prisoner. Discussing things with the others, they decided that it was risky but they had no option but to try and to hope that luck was with them and that they could find the freezing, dry, dark mist that was their way back into their lost world. It had to work, the problem was, of course, Lawson. If he managed to return with Tina and Harry, he would escape justice; if he stayed he most certainly would divulge neither to Tina nor Harry how to reactivate the phenomena. But he had promised to 'give himself up' so they could only hope he would keep his promise.

Raven-Scar or the town that never was

Another problem was PC Whitaker. If they succeeded and all three managed to go from this world back to, or more to the point forward to their world, then the Constable would be charged with a serious offence of dereliction of duty, no matter if he could explain the details. It was very possible that no one other than possibly, Detective Woods, would believe his story. Tina came up with a solution; what if they pretended that they had overcome the constable, handcuffed and gagged him and put him in the cell. At least he had the opportunity to explain that he had been attacked and placed in the cell after being knocked unconscious and it sounded like it might work. If it didn't and the three other world people could not find the way to return, at least all would not be lost, even if Lawson was recaptured and Tina and Harry arrested, they now knew what to look for.

They put this plan to Cyril who thought it might work as he would be able to say correctly that they had set a trap for him. So plan 'A' as they called it was put into motion. Cyril was handcuffed and put into the cell, gagged, so that he could not get the gag off and handcuffed to the iron bed. The cell door was locked and the key put back onto the coat hook. It was 5am and Agnes was still asleep as the plan was put into place. Lawson staggered after the two young people. Harry and Tina had previously pushed the motor-bicycle back to the Police Station, not too close but far enough away so that when Harry started the bike up it would not disturb Agnes. With the bike started and the motor ticking over they had to find the easiest way for all three to sit on it. Tina had to slide far forward on the petrol tank whilst Harry shuffled as far as he could without pushing her off; Lawson managed to cling on to the rear of the seat holding his crutches.

Harry put the bike into gear and let the clutch out and the bike wobbled forward as it gathered speed, Harry turned round and entered the road that led to the level crossing where he could make a left turn into the tunnel. The bike rattled over the sleepers nearly throwing them off. Harry found that what he had said he would do, pretend that the bike had a problem making Lawson get off of the bike, he just couldn't do it. He decided that for all his shortcomings, Lawson had told them the way back and with luck they would find out if he, Lawson, was telling the truth.

There was no way to doubt that Lawson had more to lose if he was not telling the truth; he had his life to forfeit. Harry had to make a quick decision. If he and Tina went back, then Lawson had to go with them. That of course depended on the fact that a major piece of luck was going their way. The bike hammered over the rail sleepers and rattled into the tunnel, which was not very long. They entered the dark hole of the entrance and Harry turned on the bikes headlight and the brightness lit up the whole of the tunnel. Suddenly, a dark shape appeared and the temperature dropped sharply: they all shivered with the sudden change and Lawson shouted.

'Its there thank god for that; go for it Harry for goodness sake get through it.'

Harry opened the throttle and the yellow Suzuki shot into the dark, freezing mist. They exited into a dark, early morning, with no lights showing other than the bikes headlight. The motor-bicycle stopped bouncing around; they shot past an overgrown concrete old Ravenscar Station and hurtled down the solid old rail track for half a mile until Harry stopped. Lawson slid off the back of the bike and hobbled around until he could take hold of his crutches. Harry slid to the rear of the saddle, as Tina moved herself far enough back so that she could climb off of the bike. Harry put the side stand down and looked around; all was quiet. No lights showed from where they had come and he breathed deeply and put his arms around Tina, who was shivering in the cool air. Harry rubbed her shoulders, and whispered.

'We've made it Tina we are back in our own time, thank goodness! Mr Lawson I wanted to leave you, did you know that? You killed a man and you should have faced a trial,

Raven-Scar or the town that never was

but you've escaped justice in that world, will you keep your promise?'

'Maybe Harry; maybe. Let's not be too hasty.'

'Never mind that now, for goodness sake let's get as far from here as possible, then we can think of what to do and in our case what to say. Harry what are we going to say? Our parents must be going mad with worry. I've lost track of time how long have we been gone?'

'Six weeks I think, I'm not too sure myself, let's say six weeks give or take, I honestly don't know Tina, we may be able to make our parents believe us but what evidence have we got? Apart from Mr Lawson and whether he would be believed is um! let's say stretching things too far. Honestly Tina I don't know. Let's try telling the truth and hope we get someone to accept our explanation. Mr Lawson, can I ask you, in science fiction stories when time travel is written about, time stands still and people return back to their own time without, seemingly any loss of time in their own time, is that so or are we really six weeks further on in our own time?'

'Sorry I don't understand you.'

'Is it the same time as we left or is the time like now six weeks older?'

'Oh, I see, no it's older. You come and go in I suppose if you like to call it the, real time.' So they had been away for six weeks, give or take, as far as they could tell, still now they were back in their own time they could think up some sort of explanation couldn't they?

Harry fired up the bike again and they clambered aboard. Slowly, they rode down the old rail track towards Scarborough. The track was nice and smooth, rather like a road than the old cinder track: someone must have resurfaced it and laid concrete along it, all in six weeks? The Suzuki trundled along past Staintondale Station, where old passenger carriages stood, partly as a reminder of what used to be, but also as they could see used as holiday accommodation. And the pylons for the Mono-Rail stood like sentries. It did not register that a mono-rail was there the station lights where lit. It looked very different to what they knew of it. As the bike carried them further on past The Hayburn Wyke and the few cottages standing there,,,,,, cottages there are no cottages near there, something not quite right. Harry stopped the bike they climbed off with Lawson using one crutch to support him-self.

'It doesn't feel right it's different, Tina lets go back to Staintondale Station and see if we can find the day and date, I've an awful feeling about this.' Tina followed Harry back along the track which they now realised was more of a road than a track, until they reached their destination - one of the old carriages had lights showing in the windows and the station clock showed 7 am. They could hear a slight humming noise.

Out of the dawn sky and high enough to leave a vapour trail they could make out an aeroplane. But not one they were familiar with. This was a delta shape and travelling far faster than they knew planes could go. There was no vapour trail; the delta shaped craft was still climbing and they watched as it became a dot in the blue sky. The air behind it shimmered like air does when it heats up. The station platform trembled under their feet and the mono-rail track sang with vibration as a long cigar shaped vehicle swept past at speed with a whoosh. Very little noise emanated from the vehicle, just the sound of its passing, then silence, until a voice called to them.

'Sorry you two but the 7 o'clock does not stop here; it stops at Raven-Scar though, have you got your card? I can delete this stop if you prefer it will save a bit of credit for you?'

Harry had a premonition.

'Can you tell us the date please?'

'The date certainly sir it is the 24th.'

'What month?'

Raven-Scar or the town that never was

'The month is September.'

'And the year?' Asked Harry

'Year, why don't you know the year? Have you been away somewhere? Well for your asking the year is 2009. Can I help in any other way?'

'I don't think so, thank you.'

'You can still catch the bus that goes from the road over that ridge behind the station, it is a bit of a walk mind you, but you will just be in time for the 7-30. Is that all you need to know?'

'Yes thank you very much goodbye.'

'Farewell and have a safe journey.' There was a faint click and the voice silenced. Harry guided Tina away from the station she shook herself loose from his hand.

'Are you thinking what I'm thinking?'

'What are you thinking?'

'That we have come forward in time to 2009 the correct day and date, but in the wrong world.'

'Yes that's what I am thinking. I wonder if this happened to Mr Lawson or what? Oh, blimey Tina, we are back to square one. We did go forward but not to our world, that's obvious. Did you see anyone speaking to us at the station?' Tina shook her head. 'No neither did I and the voice sounded like it came from a machine; did you think that?' Again she nodded her head. By now it was light and they could see more clearly. The mono-rail stretched down the rail line and as far as they could tell it went all the way to Scarborough. They walked back to where they had left Lawson, to find that both he and the Suzuki were gone, Tina gasped.

'That man I knew we couldn't trust him now he's gone down the track to Scarborough, and oh my goodness I've just thought what if he doesn't realise we are not where we should be. I'll bet that will be more than a surprise for him, what do we do now Harry? How long will it take us to walk back to Raven-Scar?'

'About an hour I should think, why?'

'Well there's not much point in going on is there, we might just as well walk back to the tunnel and try to find our own way back, we may be lucky that weird mist might still be there you never know.'

'Call it the probability factor' said Harry.' Come on then, let's go back or forward or whatever, I've lost track of time, and hope that there is enough charge in the batteries in either the camera or our phones to trigger the time slip, I mean what else can we call it?' He laughed at this and taking Tina's hand they turned round and started their weary way back from where they had come. The singing Mono-rail announced another carriage going in the opposite direction and the whoosh as it swept overhead startled them. No one was more startled than the woman who stepped out from the old rail carriage to see two young strangely clad youngsters walking hand in hand past Staintondale platform.

'Good morning' Harry shouted, the woman smiled and waved then stepped back into the carriage. 'Did you see what she was wearing?' he asked his companion.

The bright blue one piece garment fitted very closely to the woman's body, rather like a full length body stocking. Tina was looking behind them and suddenly she pushed Harry in the back so that he stumbled onto the grass alongside the track. The yellow Suzuki went tearing past, not stopping and disappeared into the distance, the rider with his bandaged leg sticking out.

'STOP' Harry shouted, without success. The rider carried on, oblivious to the shouting of the two stranded time travellers.

'Harry don't bother, Lawson has no intention of doing what he said, I hope he rots in hell.'

'That's a bit strong he did tell us how to find the mysterious mist, and how we think it is activated.'

'Yes but only for his own benefit, I hope PC Whitaker catches him before he disappears.'

Raven-Scar or the town that never was

CHAPTER 25

To put no finer point on the matter that is exactly what happened. As Lawson rode past Raven-Scar station monorail, he had the unfortunate experience of running himself and the Suzuki through time, unfortunately for him the time differential took him back to 1909 in the alternate world. He appeared just as the 8am to Scarborough exited the Raven-Scar tunnel with the consequence that 120 tons of steam train and three carriages destroyed the venerable Suzuki and broke Mr Lawson's other leg. PC Whitaker made an easy arrest and Lawson ended up on the train to Scarborough General Hospital. PC Whitaker asked certain questions, mainly, did Tina and Harry manage to find their own time of 2009. Lawson said he was not in the least bit interested in what happened to those two young people, they could die as far as he was concerned.

It was pointed out to him that the only person there that was almost certain to die, was himself at the end of a rope in Armley Jail in Leeds. His countenance blanched at the prospect and the bank/jewellery robber pleaded for mercy on the grounds that he was sorry and that he had not meant to kill anyone. PC Whitaker went to the trouble of saying that if that was so, then why carry the sawn off shotgun in the first place? Lawson said it was for protection. From what asked the constable? Lawson had no answer to that, and was shortly placed in the custody of Detective Woods and his subordinate PC. Lawson. He would hang; there was no doubt of that.

Tina and Harry had no knowledge of the end of Lawson. His gamble was that he could flit through time to his own advantage, but there was another law, but not one of physics; this was known as 'Sods Law' and stated that if something was probably going to happen then it most certainly will! The two old carriages at the sidings at Staintondale station were coming to life. As they stood on the platform, they heard and saw signs that food was being prepared and the smell of cooking made their mouths water. Rumbling stomachs told them that their breakfast was in the previous century, now that was confusing! They both heard the click as the information speaker came to life; the same sounding voice startled them.

'May I help you?' It questioned.

Harry's reply was in the negative, the voice once more bid them "Have a safe journey." Looking around at the station they became aware that it looked slightly familiar. Certain items reminded them of what stations used to be like, a 'bag' barrow for instance, and the station clock was an old analogue one not digital. A large advertising screen took up most of one wall, with the adverts scrolling through.

'Tina, look at that advert, it's advertising the Hover Craft ferry to Holland from Scarborough, and my god look at that, the Ferry goes to the holiday island of Dogger Bank. In our time they were going to build a wind farm there; let's see if we can find more info on the holiday island. It says that the ten mile stretch of beach is ideal for wind-surfing and that snorkelling is available. I'll bet. Also you can take a trip out to the old oil drilling platforms that were abandoned in 1992. Do you know Tina I wouldn't mind living in this world.'

'Harry, you are amazing where would you really like to live? You now have a choice, in a future 2009 of which we do not belong. A past of 1909 which we do not belong, and in which we could be accused of all sorts of things and slung into jail - not a prospect near to my heart at all! Who knows we may be travelling in time like Doctor Who forever. Harry all I want to do now is to be going home to mine and your 2009. Can we concentrate on that please? Before both of us go bonkers.' Tina knew that the nightmare she and Harry

Raven-Scar or the town that never was

were living through would only become worse, unless they found out how they could return to their 2009. Nightmares do not come more real than this she thought. Harry was not thinking too clearly, the more time they spent gazing at advertising for a holiday resort that did not exist in their time, the less time they had of returning to Raven-Scar and.

Yes that word 'and' becomes a word vital to them, the what ifs and the where ats were only words: they had to do something positive, and (that word again) that was to retrace their steps up this concrete road, back to the Raven-Scar in the past (not theirs) and hope that Lawson had not blown their chances of a quick return to the time of their birth. At twenty minutes past nine in the morning, Harry and Tina finally stopped at Raven-Scar. The station was not unlike a modern railway station, with the exception that the mono-rail platform stood twenty foot up in the air, with steps down to the original platform. They were surprised to see that the café still existed and the houses were still there. The main street still continued down to the town centre, and as far as they knew, the harbour and cliff lift still remained. They realised that they were both very cold, in fact chilled to the bone would be more accurate; rubbing their arms to help their circulation they entered the café.

The lights were on in the dining room, tables and chairs stood silent waiting for customers, sitting down somewhat puzzled, they waited. A tall, young woman came towards them her clothing looked very familiar,

'Can I help you, I'm afraid it's rather too early for our full all-day breakfast but I could fix you up some toast if you like?'

'Erm, toast and coffee would be nice please' said Harry.

'You look a bit cold, go into the other room ,the fire's lit in there.' Two cold individuals went into the warmth of the 'other' room where a fire burned in the grate - a 'real' fire said Tina. They sat as close as they could to the warmth, and their toast and coffee arrived on a tray.

'You two are out and about early, are you staying at the Youth Hostel?'

'Not exactly, but can you tell us when the next mono-rail carriage to Scarborough comes along?'

'Mono-rail, what do you mean mono-rail? There's no such thing as a monorail, the trains haven't run here since say 1960 odd, aren't you from round here?'

'Erm sort of we come from Scarborough, out of curiosity what date is it?'

'It's on the calendar over there have a look,' the waitress went back into the other room and Tina went to the calendar.

'Harry quick come and have a look at this.'

The calendar showed a view of Scarborough Castle and the date was 24th September 2009. Harry grabbed Tina's hand and more or less dragged her out of the café. They stood looking at three houses. There was an unused rail platform and a small grassed area in front of the three houses, but nothing else was there. They walked round to the end of the row and looked at open space. Apart from the odd house standing, where before a whole town had stood, there was nothing! They could see the Coastguard station and the garage for its vehicles but little else.

'Oy! You two come here you haven't paid.'

Harry looked at Tina, and laughed out loud, grabbing her and hugging her so tight she could hardly breathe.

'For goodness sake Harry let me catch my breath what's the matter with you'

'Tina we are back in our own time! Look no houses, only this road, no Police Station, no garage, no coal yard, no trains. No trains Tina, we are back in 2009 our 2009.'

'Are you sure? How can you be so sure,' the waitress was holding out her receipt for £3.50 for toast and coffee. Harry emptied his pockets of old coins and the waitress looked at them, and then at the two smiling youngsters.

Raven-Scar or the town that never was

'Come off it you two these aren't right, you know. Jeffrey come here a moment' and out of the café door strode an elderly man.

'What's up love having trouble?'

'Just a bit look at the money these two have given me, old pennies and half-pennies, call the Police Jeff, I'm not having this, they can sort this out' Jeff pulled out his mobile phone, but before he could dial Tina asked.

'Before you do that will you tell us something, have you read the paper over the past few weeks?'

'Certainly why?'

'Has there been a report of two children missing from a bike ride on the old rail way?'

'There was and the search is still going on they disappeared about six or so weeks ago. Also two other men went missing about the same time. My goodness are you two the missing kids?' Tina winced at the word kids.

'I think that we are those two. Can we use your mobile please, ours have both flat batteries?'

Jeff handed her his phone without a murmur. Tina dialled her parents land line and listened until the receiver was picked up.

'Mum it's me Tina. Yes I'm here in Ravenscar. Yes both of us. Don't cry mum we are both alright I can't tell you what happened over the phone,,,,,, yes alright we will wait here for someone. Don't cry mum, we are both alright, honestly we are, and can you tell Harry's parents please?,,,,yes thanks mum bye.' Turning to Harry with Jeff and the waitress listening open mouthed, she said. 'We have to wait here for a police car coming to fetch us. Why are you smiling Harry.'

'Tina don't you see this is where we came in? It's nearly the same, only in reverse. The mist Tina, remember, it was so cold when we went into the café. Mr Jeffrey has anyone seen two mountain bikes around here?'

'Yes this morning as a matter of fact they were found in the middle of the field over there, along with some clothing.

That was when the police said that you were most likely dead. I must say if you are the two youngsters, then you don't look much dead to me. Where have you been? The police will want to know you know, and why the old clothing?'

'It's a long story and one that we really don't know how to answer it; how are we going to answer it Tina, any ideas?' Tina shrugged her shoulders, Jeff was walking back to the café, and told them to follow him to have a look at the two bikes and the clothes. They were theirs alright, no doubt about it, but as to changing into their own clothes, they thought best not to until they had a chance to explain, explain what!, That they went through time into a parallel world! They might just as well say they were kidnapped by aliens, it would sound just as weird.

Inside the café and in the warm room Harry and Tina were left alone as the owners went about their business. Waiting for the Police they both spoke at the same time. 'What are we going to say', Tina spoke first.

'Harry, this is going to be just as bad as disappearing. I mean, how do we explain it and more to the point what do we say, when it's found out that we have been found and the papers report it. We just can't say we travelled in time and went back a hundred years to another parallel world like ours only different. People will think we are crazy. Or more likely they'll say we're two children who ran away somewhere. Or would people think we were having a game or something? What do we say?'

'Let me think Tina. At the moment I am more than relieved that we are back in our own time. I'm all for saying we had been abducted by aliens; at least we don't have to try to tell people the truth. Crikey Tina, I wonder if the photographs we took on Mr Broadbent's camera are on it or have they been erased when we came back? I've got it in my pack here. Let me switch it on.'

Raven-Scar or the town that never was

The camera lit up Harry pressed the 'ON' button and turned to the 'images' section as he scrolled through the photos on the screen he stopped.

'Yes' he breathed. 'They are all on, look the harbour, the town centre, the garage and the Police house as well. There's also the name as we found it - Raven-Scar Holiday Town. It's all there, but who do we show it to? I mean if that weird mist still exists which it must do, we have just come through it. If all this is made public we could have masses of people trying to go back in time to that alternative world. It would be chaos! Time travellers would destroy the balance of both times. It's unthinkable Tina, and I'm pretty sure it would happen. Don't you think so?'

'Yes I do, but we can't just say aliens abducted us. That would sound just as barmy as what really happened. Don't you think that we should remain silent until we have spoken to our parents, and let them make a decision?'

'Yes, I agree, that sounds like the best idea so far. I could eat another toasted tea cake could you?'

Two more toasted tea cakes and two mugs of tea later, a Police car rolled up outside of the café, two PCs entered one WPC asked how they were and where had they been. The answer was "wait please until our parents have seen us and spoken to us."

The journey took half an hour from Ravenscar. The café proprietors refused any money, and the two PCs did not ask too many questions. The two bikes were left behind to be collected later but they bundled their clothes together into a plastic bag along with their mobile phones and Mr Broadbent's camera. Fifteen minutes into the ride back to Scarborough the WPC turned to them and asked a question.

'Now you two. Call me Christine please it's much friendlier than WPC etc. I am not going to ask more than one question but this one has us puzzled. We have a problem. Can you tell us about a mystery that occurred sometime yesterday? From Ravenscar we got a call that a motorbike had crashed near the station and was severely damaged, so much so that our informant said it looked as if it had been run over by a train, any ideas?'

Tina looked at Harry and she shook her head.

'You look a little surprised. Why is that?' the WPC had a very penetrating gaze, Harry was uncomfortable.

'It's erm, well it's a little bit unusual. I mean it is very unusual, and if we said anything you would think we were acting and speaking very strangely. Look can we get to our parents first and then we can tell you as much as we can. Believe us when we say it will be a really, really weird story, true but definitely very weird.'

The WPC turned to her companion who shrugged his shoulders as much as to say leave it up to them to tell us.

One hour later both Harry and Tina were being hugged by parents, brothers, sisters and anybody else who was there. Somehow news had got out that the two children who disappeared six or so weeks ago had been found safe and well. The media, of course, had to be there and TV crews as well as newspaper reporters turned up; the two Police Constables had to force a way through the crowd, and into Tina's parents' house.

'Thank god you are safe, Tina and Harry we have been going out of our minds wondering what had happened, we thought you had been kidnapped or the very worst killed. It's been a nightmare with the papers calling it another 'Moors killing' like that chap Brady. For goodness sake you two, where have you been? It's alright if you wanted to go away together we will understand, but you should have told us. I really don't know what I am saying.'

'It's alright mum, nothing like you thought has happened to us. Just the reverse really, well not quite the reverse but, mum, can we have something to drink and a sandwich? We have only eaten some toast since last night, about 100 years ago.' Tina was feeling very mischievous. Harry gave her a stare as if to say 'don't utter a word'. Tina's

Raven-Scar or the town that never was

mother brought forth food and hot coffee, the two time travellers set to with gusto. Even the two Constables were offered a mug of tea. Harry's parents wanted to know exactly what they had been up to and Harry said they would all know when he and Tina had finished their meal. Harry's father was about to grab his son and give him a good shaking when the WPC stopped him and calmed him down.

Harry's father looked at the two children.
'You said just now something about a hundred years ago. What did you mean by that'?'
Now, the whole story had to come out with Tina and Harry taking it in turns when one or the other stumbled over their recalled thoughts. Two hours later, there was a stunned silence in the room; it was filled with parents, brothers, sisters, and the two Constables. Harry had asked the two PCs if they wouldn't mind asking non- relatives to leave the house. Some reporters showed anger at not being invited into the house and the TV crew thought they had the monopoly until WPC Christine showed she was a lot tougher than any of the crew and wanted no nonsense. Firmly but surely the two PCs cleared the house and listened in amazement to what Tina and Harry had to say. Parents interjected the explanation with 'impossible!' 'I don't believe it!' and 'it can't happen. Time travel is not possible!' and 'sorry. You two. But you are trying to cover up something that you are both ashamed of.' This last statement was from Harry's father.

Harry asked just what his father meant which made him bluster by saying 'you know'. Harry said no, he did not know; he and Tina were telling things as it happened and if he did not believe them then tough luck! He and Tina did not care what he thought. They knew that the story they told was all true. It was not a dream or a figment of their imagination, but the truth.

At this point the Policeman, who went by the name of PC Peel, spoke into his radio asking for details of missing persons in the Scarborough area, all the people in the room heard the reply quite distinctly.

'A suspected sheep stealer called Lawson has been posted as missing, whereabouts unknown. Last seen on Whitby Moors with other known sheep stealers. He escaped on a motor-cycle and was heading towards Ravenscar. Since then no sightings have been acknowledged. A Suzuki motor cycle, which has been identified as belonging to a Mr Lawson, was found very severely damaged near Ravenscar.

One other person, described as a rambler, is also missing. There has been no sign of either person for the past month and a half. The rambler's name is Mr Broadbent and was walking part of the Lyke Wake Walk, according to his wife.'

PC Peel turned to look at the gathered audience.

'I think we have to look more closely to what these two are saying. Harry and Tina, have you any evidence of what you have told us? Remember, we are trying to believe your story but to say it's far-fetched is an understatement. Can you try to remember anything at all?'

Tina and Harry shook their heads. Suddenly Hurry's older brother shouted out.

'WOW here, dad, look at this! It's a mobile phone. It's not Harry's. I've just recharged it on my charger. Look, for goodness sake this is incredible. Harry did you forget this phone?'

'Oh!, gosh yes I did. It's Mr Broadbent's phone and his camera, and we took photos with it. It was the only one that had enough charge in it to take pictures, I'd forgotten it.'

Those pictures clearly showed the name board of Raven-Scar and what was also written on it; that it was a holiday town twixt Whitby and Scarborough. Also quite clearly shown was the harbour with fishing boats, the steep steps down to the harbour and the cliff-lift; also the streets of houses, the hotel in the distance, the police house and the rail station with a smoking engine just visible. Also shown was Tina standing alongside the Suzuki after they had filled it with petrol and the garage with the Shell logo

Raven-Scar or the town that never was

behind her. Harry had forgotten he had taken that one. There was silence in the room, Tina's mother cleared her throat and whispered to no one in particular.

CHAPTER 26

'How, I mean, how did you get those photos? Are they real? Where did you take them and this Mr Broadbent, who or what is he? Did he kidnap you? I won't be angry if you just tell the truth. All that you have told us so far is pure imagination Tina. If you and Harry wanted to go away together then you've chosen a strange way to go about it. Did we, your parents, fail you in any way?'

Mrs Whitely was trying to come to terms with science fiction; something that was beyond her imagination, and the fact that, as a parent she had not noticed anything unusual about her daughter's and Harry's behaviour.

PC Peel spoke before anyone else had the chance to say anything.

'I think, Mrs Whitely you should listen to what these two are telling us. The Police have it on record that a Mr Broadbent and a Mr Lawson are on the list of missing persons. both the WPC and myself have had more of a discussion than you have with both Harry and Tina, and yes, it sounds fantastical but when I tell you that a very, very damaged yellow Suzuki motor-cycle has been recovered from near the old rail tunnel then we have to think seriously about what they are telling us.'

Harry was the next to speak.

'Mr Peel. Is that right about the motor-bicycle?'

'Certainly it is. WPC Christine will verify it.' The WPC nodded her head in agreement.

'Harry, why would the motor-bicycle be found near the tunnel? We left it in 1909 in another time?'

'That's it Tina, neither our bikes nor the motor-bicycle belong in that time and when we returned to the present day, they did also. Just like us they don't belong in 1909.'

Raven-Scar or the town that never was

'Then neither do Mr Lawson or Mr Broadbent do they? What happened to them? If they've buried Mr Broadbent he'll rise up out of the grave and Mr Lawson will escape justice won't he?' Tina was absolutely correct.

'And we went through the mist whereas the bikes haven't.' That was now a conundrum, how to explain that one! Cleverer brains than those in the house would be needed. Professor Hawkins! Even he would be stumped for an answer.

Harry's father knew the answer or so he thought. He probably did have the answer, who knows! More to the point how can it be proved, when time travel is impossible? Einstein may have the answer but seeing as he died some time ago then that idea was a dead duck. Still Harry's dad spoke up.

'I wonder if it's because the bikes are inanimate objects? Tina and Harry say they entered this strange freezing mist, Mr Lawson obviously did because they say he ran into a train or the other way round perhaps, so that could be the answer. You know the materiel and the technology does not belong there and so forth. But it's a possible answer. I may be totally wrong but it seems to me to be at least as good an explanation as we are going to get if, and I say this without really fully believing this fairy story although I may do in time, we don't have a better explanation.'

The idea was considered and because Tina and Harry had brought with them their phones and Mr Broadbent's camera, there was little point in any further consideration and it had to be agreed by all those in that room that the two young people who had been missing for a length of time were telling the truth. Another puzzle was the whereabouts of the gold coins and bullion. If, as it's thought that inanimate objects would have to revert to their origins, would this horde of precious metal suddenly disappear.

That question is purely academic as Lawson's gold is hidden and the people who are trying to come to terms with time travel, have no idea where it is. Maybe in the future it will suddenly be found and designated as 'treasure'. It's all possible of course, just like 'time travel'.

Tea and coffee was prepared again along with sandwiches and the two PCs made themselves comfortable after radioing in to the station explaining that statements were taking longer than they had expected. WPC Christine then said what all of them were thinking.

'Listen, I know I am a Police Woman and I have to uphold the law but we have a seriously strange situation here and one which will be looked on as a crackpot idea to cover up the disappearance of two teenagers. All sorts of stories will be circulated unless you can come up with an explanation which seems reasonable. Say something like the two of them have been staying with relatives and you forgot about it. I'm not saying that's it, but you must have a sensible story. Newspapers are not fools you know and they can make two and two make five very easily so thinking caps on and you have to come up with something the same as PC Peel and I. We all have to have the same story, so thinking hats on and make it good.'

WPC Christine was correct. Who would believe such a stupid story as time travel? So it was that various stories were concocted with most being rejected. The major drawback was the length of time, if it had only been two weeks then an easier explanation would have been simpler but it was the time gap that was the problem.

And the problem would be given a chance of believability but from an unusual source.

The following morning the two PCs were back at Tina's house prepared to assist in a cover up story, which had to have an essence of believability. It was going to take some time.

Both families were present, and the problem of Mr Broadbent was aired. Should they tell what happened, should they return the camera and phone with Tina's and

Raven-Scar or the town that never was

Harry's pictures downloaded onto Harry's computer? Various suggestions were made; all along the lines of forgotten holidays or visits. These were still not very good but the best they could come up with.

Mr Broadbent's equipment was another problem, it was decided to take the pictures of relevance out and forget about the man, this would pose a serious problem for the two PCs but if the explanation had to carry weight then the disappearance of two men would go down in the records as 'Missing. Whereabouts unknown.' If any problems arose from this it would be a classic case of wasted Police time.

Without warning the house telephone shrilled. They all looked at each other Mr Whitely picked up the receiver.

'Hello,,, yes it is....pardon, who are you?.... I see.... today? Now? Where are you?.... yes, hold on one moment.'

He turned to the others with a strange expression on his face. 'This person says he is Brother Jardine from the Retreat near Danby on the moors and he says he would like to speak to us, he sounds as if he knows what has happened to Tina and Harry. But how could he?'

'Tell him to come to the house, we will be here but not in this room' The WPC wanted to remain absent from the room but still able to hear what was being said.

'Hello Brother Jardine, sorry about that... Yes that would be quite alright, half an hour is fine. Looking forward to meeting you.' Replacing the phone Harry's father had an expression of puzzlement. 'How does he know for goodness sake? Not only have we a story that beggars the imagination but now we have a monk who appears to know all about Harry and Tina. Do you know something? I'm beginning to find credibility in their story. It sounds crazy I know, but this Jardine person was very persuasive.'

Brother Jardine presented himself, clad in white, wearing sandals, with a heavy looking medallion round his neck. After introductions he asked if he could speak to Tina and Harry in private. The adults were not too keen on this and neither were the two PCs, but the Father got his way. He was very persuasive.

The two children and the monk entered into the comfortably furnished sitting room, and, sitting comfortably. The monk explained the workings of his particular retreat, saying that he and his companions lived an austere life without communicating very much with the outside world. That that they took visitors in for periods of time, people of all ages and all beliefs. He smiled when Harry asked how he knew about him and Tina.

'Ahh! Now that is the question. How do I know? Let me show you something.' He reached into the small rucksack he carried and handed to them a photo. Harry and Tina gasped in astonishment, the photo showed the harbour and boats and the cliff lift at Raven-Scar.

'That, is not possible, where and how did you get this?" Harry was flummoxed.

'Would it surprise you very much if I told you I too have visited this place? A few years ago I wanted to leave my very strict order and set up my own retreat. My faith was sorely tested but I knew I could do better on my own, so I managed to purchase an old very dilapidated farmhouse, and with the help of a few companions we finally had a suitable place for our type of faith. We do not worship any deity or so-called craven images although that is an old fashioned term. No we really communicate with nature, grow our own food and run our own farm. We do not, strange to relate, have a name. People call us 'those weirdo's on the moors.' Any visitors we have stay for some while, and that is my proposal to you two; that for reasons known only to yourselves you decided to stay at the retreat,' smiling at them he carried on. 'I know only too well your problem. When I read in the paper that you had been found under mysterious circumstances, I thought of my own predicament when it happened to me. I visited your other world and was terrified but I finally found a way back, and unfortunately I had to leave my companion behind.'

Raven-Scar or the town that never was

'Companion?' queried Tina.

'Ah! Yes poor soul. Matilda failed to return with me. She insisted on staying and eating the grass.'

'GRASS' exploded Harry, 'what are you talking about?'

'Matilda was my donkey. Because I live where I do it is very isolated so I and my companions use either horses or in my case I prefer a donkey. As meditation I sometimes take a ride along the old rail track and on one occasion whilst using my phone - we monks have to keep up with modern trends you know- I entered into a very cold dark mist near to the station, the old station. Matilda and I carried on and we entered the mist and found we were in a strange place. No one I knew existed at Ravenscar, oh no, this was entirely different, so very different in fact, that I thought I had somehow been transported to a heavenly place, if one believes of course.' He said with a smile. 'So what did I make of this place? It looked somehow familiar. At least the houses did and as I rode out of the station it was obvious that the station was used. People were standing on the platform with the booking office and rooms behind them, but that was not possible as I *knew they* were not there. I knew that but there they were, it cannot be denied. They were solid buildings not a figment of my imagination. I had to be open minded and look at this phenomena through new eyes. Simply put, there had to be an explanation, and as you know that explanation is real to we who have been there, but very difficult to convey to others.'

'Why did you not make these phenomena known at least to the newspapers?'

'Tina, my child. Who would believe a crazy monk who lived a life of austerity out on the moors and was known as a 'weirdo'? You see my point and my problem? So I kept quiet. I only mentioned it to one other person when I returned without Matilda, and he suggested that I had had a vision. I thought that was a reasonable explanation on my part but unfortunately you two cannot claim to have seen such as I, can you? The Police are involved and your parents are slightly sceptical. Now can I make a suggestion? It is that you say for reasons known only to yourselves you decided to take a sabbatical at our retreat on the moors, and that for your own reasons you failed to tell your parents.'

Harry was unsure that this simple explanation would suffice. Brother Jardine said it would if they stuck to the story. He would corroborate their explanation. Their parents and the two PCs had to be confident as well in their story. 'Yes', said the Brother, 'it would work, and in a few weeks your story would be forgotten such was the short memory of the media. You would be under pressure for a couple of days but if everybody states the same story then no further discussion would be necessary.'

Returning to the rest of the family, Tina and Harry told them what Brother Jardine was prepared to do. When asked why he would do such a thing, he smiled enigmatically, saying that he knew of things that were beyond this world, and his position as a recluse, or very near, gave him a certain amount of mysticism. Even in this modern age many people were wary of a mystic, especially one who said he had a belief in the divine work of nature, here he grinned at the gathered group.

'You see, living as we do out on the moors we have a sense of difference. We are not different of course; we are just the same as anybody else but we have found by dressing in our white robes people either look upon us with a sceptical eye or are profoundly reassured by our presence. And if the newspapers dared to point a finger at us as being untruthful or acting in an illegal sense then we would consult our lawyers. They are very vigilant and will sue at the drop of a hat, which they have done in the past. One well known Sunday paper paid us handsomely when they suggested we were charlatans. Definitely not! We are not. We are a group of like-minded persons who believe in what we do. Now please, for all your sakes, discuss what I have suggested to these two young people who through no fault

Raven-Scar or the town that never was

of their own are caught up in a fantastic true tale, but who would believe them eh?'

Not one of you did so when they tried to tell you what they had been through, did you? No you did not. The story is too far-fetched. Just think what would happen to all of you if the truth did come out? Why, you would be the laughing stock of the nation, 'the people who believe in time travel', you would be the butt of every joke about weirdo's', he laughed at this. "Tell me about it. I'm a living example of being thought weird.'

Brother Jardine was true to his word. He corroborated everything that was said to the press and the TV channels, even the two PCs came up trumps they did not want to be thought weird as it could jeopardise their chance of promotion. The media soon forgot the two children who had forgotten to tell their parents that they wanted some space on their own, well not quite on their own if they went into the Moors Retreat, at Edge Farm.

The disappearance of both Lawson and Mr Broadbent, remained a problem but it was thought that it was better for all concerned to say nothing and let time heal itself. It was rather selfish they knew but apart from speaking out and being ridiculed what else could they say?

Harry and Tina were troubled by Mr Broadbent. Lawson was not on their mind he was a thoroughly bad person and was by now well and truly out of both worlds. Justice takes its toll. It was Mr Broadbent who was another matter. They decided to download all the pictures taken on the mobile and on the camera, and they still had Broadbent's rucksack. Unbeknown to any of the adults they planned to leave these items in such a place that when found it would be presumed that the poor man had somehow fallen into the sea and his body would probably never be found. They didn't know what else they could do.

That was exactly what happened. The headlines stated 'Man's belongings found on the shore at the base of dangerous cliffs.' A search for the body was put into place but a Coastguard spokesman said it was 'highly unlikely that Mr Broadbent's body would be found.'

It was the best that could happen.

Future cycle rides on the old rail track by Tina and Harry were taken with survival in mind. In case they ever slipped away into another world, they made sure both of their cameras were fully charged along with their mobiles, just in case. And if they did suddenly disappear, then their families would know where they were. Well sort of.

Time travel, never happened again to Tina and Harry, not even to Brother Jardine who became a firm friend. Tina and Harry did get some searching questions from their friends but they stuck to their story, which was that they meditated, and felt cleansed by the result.

Raven-Scar never totally went from their memories, and if truth be known they would have liked to go to that other world on the odd occasion, but time travel is not possible is it?

Or is it?

Raven-Scar or the town that never was

Printed in Great Britain
by Amazon